Key to Love

Key to Love

Much more than just a story

Edited by David L. Repsher
Scribes Valley Publishing

Book 1 – Stand-alone Novels:
Portraits of Love

Studio Seven Publishers
PO Box 41, Inglewood 4347
NEW ZEALAND
64 (06) 7568517
email: carolyn.aish@xtra.co.nz

This edition printed by
CreateSpace.com
For lovers of
Carolyn Ann Aish books,
worldwide.

ISBN 1-877219-81-9

To Christine

Chapter One

Like a sneaking reptile, Ludwig's hand slid to the jeweled hilt of his sword, then across to his dagger. He was yet undecided. It had to look like an accident. The tinkling sound of a small waterfall came to his ears. "It will head toward water, Your Highness," Ludwig whispered. *A drowning will be perfect! It will feel less like murder than it will to stab the prince*.

Tethering the two horses, Ludwig followed Prince Lothar, who moved without a sound, gently forcing his way through the undergrowth beneath the forest's ancient trees. Before their eyes, a beautiful pool unclothed itself, dotted here and there with large grayish-white rocks that seemed to rest in the crystal waters like sleeping whales.

"Wait," the prince whispered, not taking his gaze off the prey.

Ludwig's eyes, unblinking, consented only to wait for murder.

More than two minutes passed and out of the forest on the other side of the pool stepped the young buck with its first show of grand velvet.

The prince silently raised his loaded longbow.

Ludwig, unclenching his fists, decided to wait a little longer. *The deer has been provided especially for the occasion*, he thought. *The prince will drown while trying to retrieve the carcass.*

***

The thin sound of a twig crunching woke Lucy and her large blue eyes flew open. Her senses on full alert, she lay still, her vision filled by the buck, so very close, lifting its dripping nose from the water, uncertain, then jerking back, poising itself, preparing for flight. An arrow whistled across the expanse of the crystal pond and found its deadly mark—the deer's heart.

Gasping with fear and sitting up in alarm, Lucy saw the wide-eyed deer leap toward her, splashing halfway into the water, falling, dead.

A deep exclamation reverberated across the waters of her secret pool, and Lucy snatched up her muslin dress, springing nimbly to her feet. Shaking and rearranging her hair so she could see, she wondered who would dare intrude into her sanctuary, ruining her tranquility and clouding the crystal water with blood.

A second voice joined the first, "Yes, it *is* an illusion! You're right! It *is* a naiad. Pinch me, then I'll pinch you—if you'll allow me—then we'll both know if we're dreaming."

Pulling her filmy dress on and rearranging the bulky mass of her hair, Lucy tried to see the owners of the voices, but lengthening shadows created dark uninviting dimensions between the trees. Glints of golden brassards and jeweled buckles caught her eyes and she released her bound breath of fright, realizing the voices came from the other side of the pool.

The distinctive sound of cracking twigs and horses' snorts came to her unwilling ears, and she knew the interlopers had mounts.
Lucy turned to leap from the rock's edge to the bank, but the deep voice called to her, pleading, yet commanding: "Stop...beautiful naiad! Don't leave. Stay!"

Later, Lucy would not recall why she turned, only that the voice was so commanding, reverberating with domination not to be disobeyed. Her father had spoken with similar authority and no one ever defied him. She was numbed by invading memories of her father and she frowned deeply, turned mindlessly, unable to continue her first urge to escape.

Staring out across the scintillating watery expanse, Lucy saw a man. Bearing a bow as tall as he, he stepped from the camouflage of the greenery to the small space at bank's edge. There was room only for one at that place, but she could see another manly outline in the shadows behind. The hunter in view seemed arrogant and over-confident. His clothes were not at all like those worn by other hunters Lucy had seen. Her heartbeat increased as she figured him to be from another kingdom.

Lucy's gaze quickly scanned the overhanging branches around the pond, staring up at the source, hoping that others were not creeping about, seeking the crossing to her side. She drew a breath that seared her throat with panic at the thought of the arrow, released so accurately. If she were shot through, who would ever know? Who would find her here? Would she be left, helpless, in the pond, her life-blood seeping pitilessly from her? Horror and distrust eclipsed her fair face, but before she could turn to flee again, the commanding voice returned.

"Why are you so afraid? We will not harm you. Indeed, no! But such a beautiful maiden should not be lingering in the middle of the forest, alone..."

"I came to find peace...but you spoiled it for me!" Lucy accused, knowing she could never return here.

"But we will share it with you," Ludwig called warmly, his treacherous scheme forgotten. He longed to be alone with this girl.

The tone and insinuation of the man's declaration caused Lucy fright again. This time, she sprang across the narrow channel to dry land, making sure her escape route was clear. Staring at the reddening water, she then turned for a last look at the handsome man standing on the bank.

His brown curly hair was trimmed and neat. The moustache he sported was of a lighter color than his hair and sat atop a generously smiling mouth. Lucy felt her heart pounding in an unfamiliar manner. The young man's aristocratic countenance overflowed with fascination towards her.

Lucy knew she would never forget such a face. His eyes linked with hers, even from such a distance, and seemed to bind them together forever.

She shook herself in disbelief, and continued to turn away.

"Wait, please! Before you leave, fair naiad, please...tell us your name?" The young man's voice no longer commanded, but implored.

Lucy's father had been the only one who ever called her a 'naiad' and Lucy was sure, on later reflection, this was reason she paused to converse.

Summoning her courage, Lucy was encouraged by the distance between them. She demanded, "Tell me yours first."

The young man bowed and apologized, "Forgive me, fair naiad. To see you rise from the concealment of the rock, and to behold your extraordinary beauty made me forget I even owned a name! I am Lothar Charles...and this is my companion, Ludwig." He straightened up. Grasping a strong branch above him, his warm hazel eyes sparkled as he asked, "And yours?"

"Lucy," she said simply. Her hand flew to cover her pink lips and she gasped, inwardly reproaching herself for using that name.

"Lucy? Let's see, a pet name for Lucinda?" Lothar asked. At the slight shake of her head, he continued, "Lucille?"

"No!" she answered firmly, again wondering why she was lingering.

"Lucy can't be your proper name?" he asked, then offered: "Luciana? Lucella? Lucetta?"

To which she answered, "No. No. No!" Believing the two men were alone, Lucy relaxed and laughed. The sound tinkled like wind chimes across the water.

Both men drew deep breaths at the transformation. Laughter lifted every feature of Lucy's countenance, like a rare luminous butterfly, free from its cocoon, rising to greet the sun-filled blue sky. She was indeed very beautiful, and obviously unaware of her own loveliness. Lothar, completely enchanted by now, leaned out, holding to the branch with one hand. "Lucy, I declare you are the most beautiful maiden in the entire kingdom! I must become more acquainted with you, Lucy. I'm falling in love with you..."

The smile fell from Lucy's fair young face as though the butterfly was shot through its very heart while in full flight, plummeting to the earth.

With a grimace, she scoffed lightly, but loud enough for the men to hear. "Love! Love? But what is love?"

This time, Lothar laughed. His deep voice echoed across the water, but his laughter was not unkind. Remembering his mother—for the first time without deep heartache—he answered, "Love is God's gift to mankind. Love is the most needed emotion. To give love, to receive love! Really, to be without love given and received, is to be asleep, unconscious. You awakened me, Lucy!"

He saw her head shaking and continued, "Love is gentle and kind. Love is giving...love is being together." He saw her fair curls glinting with golden lights as she again shook her head. Like a cloud overshadowing the sun, a deep scowl darkened her visage. Yet even scowling, she was exceptionally exquisite.

Lothar called, "Love is this place, Lucy. The trees, the birds, the flowers, the water, and you!" He watched her draw the long ringlets back from her face, lifting them in both hands, pushing them back and seeking to secure them behind her small ears.

"Marry me, fair Lucy!" Lothar proposed in his deepest desire. Ignoring the astonished gasp emitted by Ludwig, he called again, "Please marry me, Lucy! I love you, only you!"

Reaching for her embroidered hair band hanging on a branch, Lucy trembled. The unexpected proposal, repeated, from a stranger, placed her off-balance and the band slid from her hand into the water and floated out of reach. Lucy's face drew into a grimace that, on anyone else, would have been ugly.

"Marry you?" She laughed a strained laugh and called, "How impertinent you are, sir. But I—I will *never* marry!"

"Not even the prince of Lotharingia?" Lothar called.

Lucy's face, which mirrored self-rejection, returned to its frown of fear and her darting eyes again scanned the path of flight, to ensure that no intruders lingered there. She reminded herself of her safety, the distance separating them, and retorted, "Even less, if *you* were such a person. And besides, if you are the prince, then you would never want to marry me!"

Amazed beyond verbalizing, Ludwig swallowed. Finding his voice, he stammered, "Be—behold! She...she spurns Prince Lothar. She spurns the son of King Lothar the Third!" Under his breath, he muttered, "If she does not want him, maybe I can make her want me. Such beauty, such youth, such innocence."

The prince, bowing again, called, "My heart is yours, Lucy of Lotharingia. I must know more about you. Should I speak with your father?"

"I have no father!" she exclaimed with a resentful scowl. "And his name would cause you and *your* father to spit! If you are son of the king, then I must leave. You do not know me!" Without a backward glance, Lucy merged with the tree trunks, her white dress becoming anonymous in the deep shadows.

With great alacrity, the men rushed to gather the reins of their horses, leading them swiftly toward the pond's source, seeking a place to cross.

After searching the spot where Lucy vanished to no avail, Lothar slashed off a long branch with his sword. Stepping across to the large rock, he reached out with the branch and retrieved the floating hair band. Wringing the water from the delicately colored cloth, he examined its embroidery thoughtfully. Mounting up, they directed their horses to follow the rarely used one-horse track from the hidden haven.

Later, having ridden around the perimeter of the forest, they came across a bent widow-woman carrying a large cane basket. Ludwig dismounted and confronted the old crone.

"Did you see a young maiden wearing a white dress? She had long golden hair."

The gray-haired widow, who had an ugly hump between her shoulders, was so hunched she could scarcely look up at the man who questioned her. With a rasping voice, she said eagerly, "Yeah. I see'd 'a." Pointing her covered hand—a soiled sleeve, much too long, hid her fingers—the woman cackled and said, "She went thet-a-ways, she did. She wa' runnin' too...affrighted, I'm a-thinkin' she were...runnin' like the devil were at 'er 'eels! "

Prince Lothar reined his horse about, galloping off in the given direction.

Ludwig turned to the woman and said, "If you see her again, report secretly to me. I'm Sir Ludwig. Give any soldier a verbal message that—the Gray Hawk has news for Sir Ludwig—and I will come and see you personally. There'll be a handsome reward for you if you help me find the maiden." He tendered a silver coin to the woman, asking, "Do you understand?"

Nodding her covered head fervently, so that Ludwig could see the matted gray beneath, the woman snatched the silver ducat from his fingers so fast he did not see her hand. Swiftly mounting, Ludwig followed the prince's path.

The widow's directions led Lothar straight into his escort, the very men he and Ludwig had escaped from less than an hour ago.

Laughing at the Chief Brigadier's thunderous face, the prince said, "Oh, there you are, Marty. We wondered where you'd gone." Ignoring the angry looks from the other men of the company as they drew up behind the leader, the prince raised the blue hair band above his head.

"Ludwig and I have just seen the most beautiful maiden in the kingdom," he said as every man stared spellbound. "But, alas, she eluded us and disappeared like a nymph of the forest. Five gold ducats to the man who finds her for me. She wears a white dress and has the longest golden hair of any maiden ever seen."

At a signal of affirmation from the Chief Brigadier, the company issued happy shouts and jubilant cries, all hoping to gain the five ducats and dispersing in various directions.

The prince interested in a young maiden! Until this moment he had been interested only in hunting, target shooting with the newly designed crossbows, his horses and racing them, or riding aimlessly throughout the kingdom. How pleased his aged father, King Lothar, would be if they could find the maiden who had caught the prince's eye and captured his heart.

Lothar joined the search, but Ludwig, together with two captains, remained with the Chief Brigadier. Ludwig told them of the strange encounter with the young maid in the forest, her words, the offer of marriage blurted by the usually controlled prince, her denial and refusal, and the strange words about her father.

Marten, the Chief Brigadier, hoped his brigade would not find the coveted girl. It was of grave concern to him that the heir to the kingdom desired a maiden and was speaking of marriage. Marriage could mean an heir. And, such an heir would stand in the way of his own plans for the kingdom.

Speaking secretively to a certain few of his trusted men, the chief offered ten gold ducats to anyone who could capture the maiden and keep her out of the prince's presence.

"I'll decide what to do with her when she has been successfully seized," Marten said frowning, and then grinning.

They searched the forest, even moving inwards and hunting around the secluded pond. But there was no sign of the fair Lucy. They then looked for the old hump-backing widow in black, intending to question her further, but she, too, had disappeared.

The prince had only the costly hair band to console himself that Lucy had not been a spirit, but a real person.

Returning to the palace, miles away across country, the prince described the encounter to his father, who joyfully appreciated the value of his son's interest in a young maiden. The king had thought the day would never come! So many lovely ladies had been presented at court, but the prince had not been interested. In fact, he had been ill mannered and impatient.

Had it not been for the king's orders that the prince always be accompanied by Ludwig and surrounded by vigilant bodyguards, Lothar would have spent all his time alone in the woods, riding and hunting.

"This... maiden. Lucy, you say?" the king asked his son with great sentiment, "You'd marry her?" At the light in his son's eyes and the smile on his lips, the king commanded, "Then find her. Bring her here so we can become acquainted. Indeed! Yes, we must learn her full name. If she's as beautiful as you describe, then many will have seen her. Hair almost down to her knees, you say...golden curls. Yes, and this hair band is not one belonging to a pauper..."

He smiled, enjoying the light of romance in his son's eyes. The prince had not been interested in any female since his mother died eight years ago, when he was eleven. He had grieved for his mother deeply, inconsolably.

"It will be simple. Indeed, it will," the king declared, striding to a wall map. Pointing, "Here is the forest where you saw this Lucy. There are three villages in the vicinity. Send four brigades to search for her. She has another name, of course, but if she's known as 'Lucy' then she'll not be difficult to locate. We'll find her tomorrow."

***

Lucy had seemingly disappeared off the face of the earth. After two days of fruitless searching, instead of becoming disheartened, Lothar became more determined. He was, however, unaware that others just as determined—and offering a larger reward for information—sought to apprehend the young maiden.

Prince Lothar decided to turn the search towards the hump-backed widow, believing she knew something of the fair Lucy. He received reports of sightings of the old crone from far and near. Several widows were confronted, detained, and questioned, but none had the ugly hump and the raspy voice.

Village criers shouted descriptions of both Lucy and the widow. It was voiced that information regarding either person would bring a handsome reward, which grew larger each time it was published.

Nearly every one in Lotharingia watched and hoped that they would be the lucky subject to discover the whereabouts of these two women and make the coveted report to a local brigadier. The air was tense with excitement, but also confusion as to who wanted Lucy most: Prince Lothar, Sir Ludwig, or the Chief Brigadier.

Where was the illusive, mystical 'Lucy'?

Chapter Two

Giggling nervously from the achievement of arriving safely, Lucy opened the squeaking door and entered her home, such as it was. Closing the door and leaning on it, Lucy gave way to her emotions. The peculiar sound of her irrepressible laughter caused those in the one-room house to gasp in surprise and delight. Lucy laughing? How long had it been since they had heard this welcome, musical sound?

Lucy's cousin, Yolanda, an emotionally introverted girl of twelve, looked up as the familiar figure entered. Lucy shook the black hood from her head, pulling off the restrictive mask and gray wig. Tossing her head to release the hump of hair, she laughed loud and long. Skip-dancing about the limited floor space, her laughter had a triumphant ring.

Yolanda's eyes grew wide at the rare sound of her cousin's merriment and the sight of mirth upon Lucy's radiant face. To the surprise of those in the room, Yolanda began to giggle! No one could remember hearing the normally silent Yolanda laugh before, and they stared, spellbound; except for Avalyn, Yolanda's sister, who was blind.

The diligent Avalyn had been stirring stew in the cauldron, but at the sound of Lucy's gaiety, she left the heat of the fire, fearing if she too began to laugh, she may burn herself. Avalyn could remember being happy like this maybe once or twice before, but that was when her mother and father were alive. She knew that such laughter did not depend upon circumstances and one could be happy in both adversity and prosperity. Seeing the former was now their portion, Avalyn had never found the elusive secret by which to couple poverty with happiness.

With arms up-stretched, ten-year-old Avalyn moved towards the sparkling merriment. Grasping the light-hearted Lucy around the neck, she lifted one hand to feel the sound of Lucy's laughter with her fingertips. But, as Avalyn's gentle fingers moved up Lucy's throat, towards her lips, the laughter faded and died.

"What is it?" Lucy asked, her eyes on Avalyn's serious face. Escaping the girl's clinging hands, Lucy saw tears forming in the brilliant blue of Avalyn's unseeing eyes.

"I...I wanted to...to feel...your...laughter," Avalyn answered. Tears spilled down her cheeks.

Lucy ruffled Avalyn's blonde curls, saying gruffly, "We all should laugh much more."

A picture of the young man's face formed in Lucy's mind, but it was not clear; the lake stood between, with its rose-stained water. She thought of the deer and how good it would have been to bring the venison home. Avalyn's tear-stained face focused again and Lucy said seriously, "I should not be laughing. What I laugh about won't place food on our table!"

Swallowing at remembrance of the claim that he was the crown prince sounding out across the water, Lucy shrugged away her bleak feeling of loss, blinking, preventing unbidden tears from forming.

She seldom laughed, but she wept even less. *The young man may want me, but he would never want to take on the responsibilities of my cousins and Cynthia,* she decided, and closed the curtains in her mind on the scene at the pool and the recurring and irritating thoughts of how many meals that venison would provide.

She looked across at Cynthia, asking, "Where's Tage?"

"He's still chopping wood. Donal came and demanded another cartful. He wants it tomorrow," Cynthia answered and ceased working on the fine sewing. She asked, "What made you laugh, Winnie?"

Lucy bowed her head, unable to prevent herself from smiling. Indeed, she scarcely knew what had made her laugh; other than she had foiled the young man who sought to question her further. Her smile disappeared as she allowed her mind to return to her preconceived opinion of men: *Liars! They are all liars! That Ludwig—he's not the prince's friend. A liar, like them all!*

To her consternation, she found the curtains opening again, and her mind suggested that one man was different. Before she could halt the thought in flight, it flitted like a butterfly, saying, *He was rather princely and very handsome. His voice was deep and commanding like Father's. He called me a naiad...a beautiful naiad. And, he said he was in love with me! Love?*

Cynthia expected an answer, and Lucy realized she must not let her cousins know about *him*.

"It was my disguise...it helped me out of a difficult situation," Lucy replied, and then said gravely, "It's a good disguise, is old Widow Winnie. Who would imagine my real age, or what I really look like? But it proves how important it is that I wear such a convincing disguise. We would not get very far in the world today if I went about as Lucy. Lucy is too...too...yes, too young...and, Cynthia, your wisdom has proved right again."

At the older woman's disconcerted stare, Lucy said, "My disguise saved me from being accosted by two strangers...two strong young men."

Moving close to Cynthia and turning her head from Yolanda's vision, Lucy whispered in the nanny's ear, "They saw me before I put the mask and wig on, and they.... one of them wants to marry me, Cinnie. Don't tell the children. The other one, he said his name was Ludwig. He...he gave me this..." The silver ducat sparkled enticingly, nestled secretively in her cupped palm.

Lucy shuddered and whispered again, "Ludwig gave me the creeps..." She closed her eyes, wondering if the other man, Lothar, would make her feel that way if he were close enough to tender her a coin.

Cynthia, dropping her handiwork, stood, her mouth agape.

Ignoring Cynthia, Lucy turned and asked, "Where's Jaybee?" then answered for herself, "With Tage, I guess."

Gathering the fabric and shaking it gently whilst she nodded, Cynthia said, "Well, I'm glad you got back safely, that I am. I told you, didn't I?" The woman frowned at the two young faces turned her way. Lucy was right. Such matters could not be discussed in the presence of the children. "Y're right, Jaybee is loading the cart, helping Tage, doin' her bit like as usual. Donal wants the wood afore noon..."

"He would," Lucy said grimly. She strode to the cauldron, and stirred for a moment. "I have some *good* news. I'll share it when we're all together, after our meal."

The sun had set when fourteen-year-old Tage and six-year-old Jaybee entered the room to partake of the rabbit stew and bread that evening. Both had washed in the creek and came shivering from the refreshing water. Tage limped to his place on one of the two benches, followed by Jaybee. At their appearance, Yolanda began dishing the stew into thick pottery bowls.

The meal eaten, the table cleared, and the dishes taken care of, Lucy gathered her family around her. Lucy and the children settled on the thin rug close to the fire, the only source of light and heat, while Cynthia sat on the one chair they owned. Sleepy, Jaybee curled up, sucking her thumb, her head on Lucy's lap.

"I have a new home for us," Lucy declared with great satisfaction. She could tell her words had not sunk in; they all thought she was telling a story. "I'm told it has two side-rooms as well as the living room." She looked across at Tage and added, "There's a bed-chamber you can have to yourself, Tage. The other will be large enough for us all to sleep in. It sleeps six."

Lucy looked around the cluttered room in great disdain, saying, "I'd like to leave at first light tomorrow, but we'll have to wait until the wood is unloaded before we can pack our things on the cart. We'll leave the next morning at dawn. It will..."

Everyone, excluding Yolanda, interrupted at once, exclaiming and questioning. Lucy shared their excitement and sought to answer their many questions.

"It will take us all day to travel to Verdun. Yes, Avalyn, Verdun is the Capital City of Lotharingia. No, our cottage is not right in the city, but close to a Grand House on the outskirts.

"Yes, it has its own well, and a creek nearby. And no, it's not even as costly as this hovel. We won't have to worry about Donal and his never-ending demands for free wood. How do I know about it? Well, it's a long story."

She explained, "One of the ladies we've been taking our embroidery to—Countess Dominique—well, I made friends with one of her servants and, to condense the story, this woman-servant has a sister who works at the residence of Lord Tullus. She told me that we could have the cottage, because the lady there wishes us to sew for her. Evidently, Lady Tullus has six daughters and only one son. There will be embroidery to keep us busy without all the fuss of having to travel far or set up a market stall. And Tullus Hall has need of a full-time woodcutter." She looked at Tage, then up at Cynthia with shining eyes, saying, "It's exactly what I'd hoped for, and if we can get settled before winter, with enough work..." Lucy interrupted her own thoughts by saying, "and there are markets in the city every day of the week save one...think of the possibilities!" Sleep was slow to conquer those in that humble chamber that night.

Tage lay on a mat at the base of the door, twisting and turning, not from discomfort, but from excitement. *The city! Oh, how wonderful! To live near the city... the markets... the puppet shows... the pies... the city, the city.* He then prayed, *Please God, let it be you who leads us there. And help Lucy find the key to unlock her heart to love, especially your love...*

The girls, curled up like three kittens on the mat by the fire, snuggled close to each other, whispering quietly, not heeding Cynthia and Lucy's alternate warnings to go to sleep or they would be too tired to pack and much too tired to travel.

Lucy tried to imagine what it would be like to travel so far with a middle-aged woman, a lame boy, a voiceless girl, another who was blind, and dear little Jaybee, who had the trusting mind of a baby. *And I am an old lady,* she thought, suddenly feeling as though she was indeed. *Sometimes I feel eighteen going on forty! The responsibilities of my little family with all their needs...* She sighed and the sound was much louder than she intended.

"Will we still have to keep calling you Winnie?" a soft voice called.

Lucy pulled the curtain back from the makeshift alcove where she slept on a straw mattress with Cynthia. Striding to the fire, she threatened, "You will *always* call me Winnie. I have no other name, do you hear? You're not to ask any more questions, Avalyn. Go to sleep, all of you!"

As Lucy curled up on the mattress again, she remembered. Was it just this afternoon she had answered that young man; the one who said he was a prince? She had told him her name was Lucy. *I was Lucy... then...and I am now...but I must only be seen and known outside our family as Winnie... Widow Winnie.*

Chapter Three

The momentous move from the small village of Passcau to the city went smoother than Lucy could have dreamed. Tage had taken the wood to Donal and returned with the cart, which they loaded with their meager, well-worn possessions: rugs and a few linens, thin straw mattresses, two benches, a table, the chair, cooking pans, and six bowls.

Precious embroidery threads and sewing needles were packed in a small wooden chest with valuable fabrics, ribbons, laces, and buttons. They wore the only clothing they owned; that is, save the old locked trunk full of Lucy's wigs, make-up, disguises, and widow-wear. Both Cinnie and Lucy believed that the disguises were their survival.

Lucy had dressed in gray, the shade worn by younger widows just out of their mourning time. She matched the black sash and lace of her dress with a black wimple, worn over her hair, fixed with a see-through veil over her eyes and nose. Her slim figure made her appear frail.

Chattering loudly with both excitement and apprehension, Avalyn, Tage, and Jaybee traveled with Cynthia on the back of the cart, whilst Lucy walked, taking turns with Yolanda, leading Mortimer, the donkey, along the path towards the capital. Tage, as usual, grumbled about his lame leg, longing to be able to lead the donkey like a man, but denied this privilege due to the pain his uneven gait caused him.

An hour after leaving Passcau, the narrow lane joined with the main road to Verdun and very soon the wide route became busy. Companies of infantry, cavalry, travelers of all kinds, and varied vehicles passed the rickety cart and its female escort; some moving west, but most moving east towards the capital.

Lucy thought of the note she left tacked on the door of the 'home' they had left. She had paid Donal in advance through the end of the month so he could not complain that they left without warning him. Shuddering involuntarily, Lucy felt glad she never allowed

Donal to see through her disguise. He was a man she disliked vehemently.

So lazy, dirty, and rude, just like all men, Lucy told herself as she walked. A small voice added, *Except perhaps...**him**!* She could not rid her mind of the earnest face of the man calling himself 'Lothar Charles'.

A company of officers approaching from behind captured Lucy's wandering attention and she steered the donkey to the side of the road. Instead of passing their vehicle, the captain spoke to Cynthia, Tage, and Avalyn. Lucy held the donkey's bridle, waiting, straining to hear the man's questions. Bending her head downwards, Lucy strove to conceal her inward fright as she caught the latter half of their conversation.

"No. There's no one we know what uses that name," Cynthia said. "Lucy? Who is she?"

The leader stared at the travelers, visually combing the belongings in the cart, raking his eyes over Lucy's form as though searching for hidden weapons. "Move on!" he commanded his horsemen.

Before Lucy could inquire, Tage hissed at her, "They asked if we know a Lucy—a maiden about eighteen with long hair like Avalyn's. So what do you say to that, Widow Winnie?" His tone was teasing, and his eyes crinkled with laughter. Teasing Lucy made him feel he had power over her.

"But whatever for?" Cynthia asked fearfully, "They was cavalry...military...like those I saw once in the Royal Guard. What would they want with...with a Lucy?"

Lucy encouraged the donkey into its reluctant walk again, ignoring the chatter of her charges. *Indeed!* she thought, *what a to do. But then, it will soon be over and they won't find Lucy. No, they must never find Lucy!* Shuddering, she forced herself to walk faster, *No one shall find Lucy! I'm so glad we're moving.*

***

Verdun's city walls lay ahead, and from their vantage point, the weary travelers saw that the large city stretched a long distance. The sun sank lower and Lucy prodded the weary donkey into action, drawing him down a road along the north side of the walls. Before long, Lucy took a turn back towards the west, shading her tired eyes. The angle of the sun, combined with dust rising from the road, made her feel extremely agitated. She could smell the dust and taste its grittiness. It dragged in the hem of her gown and clung to her cloak. *Just a little walk along this lane and up that hill,* she thought, *I'm glad to be almost there. Soon, they'll never find Lucy.*

A crested signpost declared *TULLUS HALL*, and Lucy knew they had arrived.

"There it is!" Tage shouted triumphantly, pointing as they mounted a small rise. The road wound down into a valley where the Grand House rose proudly amidst prolific leafy and flowering trees. Several stone cottages nestled here and there in the valley.

"Ours is the closest, I was told. See? The smallest one with the thatched roof, among those trees, near that little creek," Lucy said, expelling a sigh in relief. She had hoped this cottage would be real, and here it was. "Peony, the servant-woman, described it well. If it's unlocked, we won't go to Tullus Hall until first thing tomorrow. Then we'll seek Peony's sister, Belva, and find out about the work that's awaiting us."

She smiled, thinking gladly, *A new life and we're together. Who says Widow Winnie can't look after a family? She can do anything. And Lucy will be a secret forever.*

Everything about the cottage delighted the newcomers. Having lived in Donal's shack for almost two years, it was like moving into a mansion. To their surprise, it was semi-furnished, the furniture newer and nicer than anything they could recall. The oval wooden table had six bentwood chairs and two stools around it. Lucy wondered what they would do with their own table and two benches. When Tage suggested they could be placed outside under the walnut tree, Lucy was delighted with the idea.

It was late when they finished unpacking and placing their shabby belongings. Their rugs looked threadbare on the polished wood floor, and Lucy determined that when she had time, she would inquire at the market and order new ones. "My savings will be well spent. We'll be happy here; we can live here for years."

The bread and cheese brought with them was stale, but everyone was glad to have supper and washed it down with cool well water. Large candles, new in their holders, were lit and a warm, friendly glow cast—*Welcome!*—to every corner.

Tage, fascinated to have his own room, examined the large four-poster bed that seemed big enough for them all. He came to the table most reluctantly, wishing he could rest on the bed instead. Later, still eating, Tage excused himself to investigate and arrange his meager belongings in his very own bedchamber, and to read a book from the bed's headboard shelf.

The built-in wooden beds in the other room had mattresses on them and Cynthia declared with certain delight, "They was aired today, I can tell. Someone has been here and prepared for us. It feels like a cozy little manor house of our very own. The lady will be agreeable to work for."

She was like a mother hen inspecting a nest of spun gold, cackling happily about every nook and cranny, exclaiming about the niceties that made this place a luxuriant lodging.

Avalyn slowly and meticulously felt her way about the rooms, gaining her own sight of the cottage, whilst the others ran rampant, touching everything, opening and closing doors that did not squeak, trying the key in the lock on the one outside door, opening and closing heavily-waxed wooden shutters.

"Tell us about the Grand House where we used to live," Jaybee demanded. The girls gathered around Cynthia and Lucy, listening and watching as Cynthia described the multiroomed Melville mansion where they all used to live. Lucy had rarely seen her father as he was employed on business for the king. As far as Lucy knew, her mother had lived a life of her own, returning rarely to visit her daughter or husband.

Mother was in Cher when it was raided. What bad timing! Of all the times she chose to visit us, Lucy thought, sighing and watching

Yolanda. The girl concentrated closely, as if lip reading Cynthia's animated monologue. Lucy knew this would be difficult by candlelight. She stared at Yolanda's face, wondering how "deaf" her cousin truly was.

In the second Cynthia drew another deep breath, Lucy stood, interrupting and commanding, "Bedtime! Everyone to bed! Tomorrow we have to present ourselves at the house and we must not look tired and worn out or they won't let us live here and work for them at all."

***

Ringing the bell at a small side door, Lucy hoped she had chosen the servants' entrance and that a simple servant would attend them. Tullus Hall also had a back door; perhaps she should have entered there?

A large footman wearing distinctive scarlet and white livery opened the door. Stepping backwards, Lucy was unable to conceal her fright. The scarlet uniform unnerved her, and she trembled, struggling to regain her composure.

"Please...we wish to see the servant-woman...Mistress Belva." Lucy saw the footman look her up and down as though trying to reconcile her young, frightened voice with the widow-woman's attire. In her trepidation, Lucy had not disguised her voice. She knew her voice surprised people, it sounded much younger than she looked.

She shrugged and inwardly remonstrated herself, *I must remember to put the croak into my voice!*

The wordless footman, surprised to hear a servant speaking in an educated voice, disappeared and the six were left standing upon the steps, waiting.

Then, a tall, slender servant-woman, wearing a distinctive dark-blue costume with a white frilly lace apron and cap, appeared at the door, asking, "Yes—what are you wanting here?"

Lucy extended her hand, saying, "Good morning, Mistress Belva. I am Winifred. Your sister arranged for us to come and work here. We arrived at the cottage last evening and felt most welcomed by the freshness of it, thank you." Again Lucy noticed the odd stare she received. She added, "I-I am a widow...and I-I haven't always had to work...like this."

Belva nodded, her eyes scrutinizing Cynthia and the children. "Peony told me. We had the cottage unlocked and aired. I'm sure you'll find it to your liking. These are your children?" she asked.

Lucy read doubt on Belva'a face. "I'm their aunt. My sister's children." Lucy felt little pressure on her conscience as she retold the lie she had been telling for over three years.

"Come in, then. We'll go to the office where you'll be formally engaged. Take the first door on the left." Frowning, she asked, "You say you've already moved into the cottage? We thought you were coming yesterday and that you would check in here first. Never mind, come along." Belva stared at Tage, taking in his limp. She craned her head, searching the grounds as though expecting someone else. Then, staring directly at Cynthia, she asked, "Where's your husband?"

Cynthia's eyes grew wide and she shook her head. "I haven't got one," she answered indignantly. "And I never had one."

"Then..." Belva looked at Lucy "...where is the wood-cutter? I was led to believe..." She stared at Tage's back as he disappeared into the office. "Come, we will sort this out with Sinclair."

The children filed into the room, followed by Cynthia, Lucy and Belva. An over-powering man sat behind a large desk and his eyes brushed them briefly, lingering on Lucy's costume, the same shabby gray cloak she'd worn yesterday. She knew it was extremely unattractive: a worn, travel-stained mass of pleats that made her appear larger than she actually was.

What she didn't know was that to the more than casual observer, her wide-set and wrinkle-free bright blue eyes did not match the reddish-gray hair protruding from her bonnet. Despite charcoal make-up lines etched and blended across her forehead, she still had the appearance of a young maid grown old before her time, her petite, heart-shaped face conflicting with the bulky, womanly costume.

This widow-woman is not what she appears, the studious Sinclair determined, considering himself astutely able to assess people's character. *She has a falseness about her, but not dishonest. I wonder what, or who, she is.*

"Sit down, sit down," he commanded, waiting. They all sat, save Tage and Belva. Sinclair drew a piece of paper from a pile on the desk. Looking up, he said, "We have Widow Winifred, Madam Cynthia, and Mistress Yolanda, all who do fine sewing?"

Lucy, being the one who always spoke for the rest, answered. "Sir, that's not quite correct. Peony must have conveyed it a little wrongly. I am Widow Winifred. Only Mistresses Cynthia and Yolanda do fine sewing. Yolanda also does beautiful embroidery as do I..."

"And the wood-cutter?" Sinclair raised his thick eyebrows and stared looked at Belva. Lucy saw that his ill-concealed annoyance was fast changing to anger.

"Tage is the wood-cutter. He works as well, if not better, than any grown man." Lucy spoke defensively.

"In *your* opinion, Widow Winifred. *We* will ascertain what the lad can do..." Sweeping his eyes across the children, he said firmly, "But you cannot have the cottage. It's for a married couple with children. That's what we understood you were..."

Lucy blinked hard. This was not as she had hoped at all. She stood and declared, "But surely, sir, if we can do the work you require, then..."

Sinclair slapped his palm on the table and Avalyn and Jaybee both jumped. "Just who do you think you are, Madam? Sit down! *I* do the employing at Tullus Hall...and I'll not tolerate you questioning my procedure." He waited, expecting Lucy to challenge him again.

Her blue eyes, stormy, engaged his, glaring, declaring war. Inwardly, she alienated Sinclair to her predisposed coffin for all men. However, remembering the cottage and their need for food and shelter, she sat and held her tongue.

Silence stole over the office chamber, continuing for several minutes as Sinclair, bringing his hands together and letting each finger meet its twin, eyed the prospects one by one.

Speaking in a calmer tone, he said, "Let's go over the proposition. Maybe we can place some of you." He frowned, obviously thinking deeply, now tapping his fingers erratically on the desktop.

"Madam Tullus is most desperate to acquire a seamstress and she is pressing me to find one—or two—to do fine embroidery..." Belva said, but was silenced with a withering glare from Sinclair.

"I'm well aware, Belva. I know exactly what Madam Tullus requires, thank you." Sinclair continued tapping his fingers, again looking around at the children.

"There are two of you who can do nothing," he announced the obvious, having noted Avalyn's flickering blind eyes and small Jaybee, who was clinging to Lucy's arm, sucking her thumb as though afraid the man would steal it from her.

"Avalyn and Jaybee help with the meals," Lucy said softly. She indicated Yolanda by touching her gently. "I must tell you, sir, that though Yolanda does beautiful handiwork, she is somewhat...impaired in her hearing..."

Sinclair raised his eyebrows, and then closed his eyes, exasperated. Rubbing his left eye with his forefinger, he asked, "Deaf? **How** deaf?"

Frowning, he glared at Yolanda, his eyes wide open like a satisfied owl eying a distant rodent. "Are you deaf?" His countenance changed a little at her nod. She had the look of intelligence and he realized she had followed their conversation.

Lucy explained, "Something happened to her four years ago, sir. She lip-reads very well, but does not speak. I...I taught her to read and write. When necessary, she communicates her needs by writing them down."

"You taught her to read and write?" Sinclair asked, and he blinked, eyeing Lucy as though she was a worthwhile individual after all.

"We all read and write, save Cynthia," Lucy said, tilting her chin. Knowing Sinclair expected an explanation, she obliged: "We all lived together in a Grand House until four years ago. My husband was killed in the battle at the border east of Cher..." Lucy saw Sinclair lean forward, his eyes fixed on her, interested in her story.

She continued in a soft voice, knowing by the change on Sinclair's face that she had his attention. "The children's mother and father were killed in a raid on Cher. We...we managed to escape, but we all bear emotional scars from that dreadful attack. I...I was the only one of us six who was not injured."

A deep silence captivated the office chamber and Lucy waited a few moments before continuing. "As you can imagine, we all had good tutors while we lived at the Grand House before the raid." Realizing she had said "we", Lucy quickly added, "I have taught the children since then...and we have fended for ourselves..."

"That was a dreadful affair!" Sinclair declared sympathetically. "It must have been terrible for you. I myself had a brother killed in defense of Lotharingia. Of course, the king couldn't let them have the village...though they've always claimed that Cher belongs to them!"

He looked up at Tage, asking, "Is that how you became lame?"

Tage nodded and spoke for the first time, "My sister Avalyn was struck on the head, that's why she is blind." He looked at Jaybee and said softly, "Jane-Belle was badly injured by a sword. Yolanda suffered great shock and lost her speech and her hearing, though perhaps not all of it."

Lucy bowed her head. She hated to recall any part of that horrific time and wanted to blot it from her memory. Any physical reminder of the battle itself caused panic to rise within her, stripping her of every vestige of reason. And now, finally, she had dared to move even further away from her home village of Cher, hoping to rid herself of the past and begin life anew.

She looked up to find Sinclair staring intently at her.

"It is against convention to allow you to live in the cottage for obvious reasons, Widow Winifred." As though sensing she did not understand or agree, he added, "A defenseless group of women and a boy? No. The master will not allow it."

Disappointed beyond expression, Lucy stood to take her leave of this man. As she opened her mouth, he spoke again, commanding that she sit and listen to his proposition.

"We have servants' quarters here in Tullus Hall. I suggest we place some of you on trial. We urgently require a seamstress and an embroiderer...and we will give the lad a chance to show himself at the wood pile." He saw mutiny glowering in Lucy's eyes and added encouragingly, "The terms are that room and food are part of the payment. The two women will receive one silver ducat each month as wages. The woodcutter will receive four silver ducats, that is, if he works like a man. Otherwise, his wage shall be reduced. I'm sure you'll find the accommodation at Tullus Hall most comfortable, and the menu exceptionally adequate. As upper servants, the cleaning of the bed-chambers will be done for you."

He waited for Lucy's answer. Every pair of eyes in the room turned to look at her.

Standing and straightening her back primly, Lucy said, "Please permit us some time to consider, perhaps until tomorrow, sir. I trust we may stay at the cottage tonight? We'll pack our things in the morning and bring you our decision. Some of us may decide to stay here, while the rest of us will seek other accommodation."

Sinclair stood and said, "I understand you need time to consider. You had your mind set upon something that's just not possible here on the Tullus Estate. You may stay at the cottage until tomorrow." He was going to add that the cottage must be left as it was found, but he knew that this strange widow would certainly take care of that. *She is a lady...not a servant,* he thought.

Speaking impulsively, he said, “I know of a place needing a teacher who can teach children to read and write. They pay well, a live-in position. And maybe, yes, the rest of you could find accommodation there. It is for people and children like you.” His face relaxed as he saw the interest in Lucy’s eyes. “I shall investigate the whole matter for you.” He bowed shallowly.

Looking into Lucy’s eyes, he said, “I look forward to your return tomorrow morning. We’ll discuss the alternatives then.”

Chapter Four

The children's chatter irritated Lucy. She wanted to think, so she set a swift pace back to the cottage, causing the others to lag behind. Lucy had always known that she could not hold onto this family, but feared for their future. Often, she had longed for freedom from the intense responsibility she had assumed in caring and providing for her cousins. Now, the skills she had taught them, with Cynthia's help, could be put to good use.

Her heart leapt as the cottage came in view. Since fleeing from the Grand House, the center of the battle in Cher, a little cottage such as this had been Lucy's dream; a secure dwelling with enough room for them all, yet not so large they would require servants to keep it. Now, this dream was shattered.

Lucy strove to view the coming separation in a positive light. It would be much better—and safer—for Cynthia and Yolanda to live in the Grand House. Cynthia would certainly take care of Yolanda. And Tage would be there.

Lucy would have Avalyn and Jaybee...and yet, maybe not. Sinclair obviously had an idea.

Once at the cottage, they made the decision to press on and grasp every opportunity that presented itself. Both Tage and Yolanda were excited about living in the Grand House and in their enthusiasm they treated lightly the coming separation.

The loss of the cottage would soon be forgotten, Lucy realized. She watched Avalyn curl up on the thick floor rug and fall asleep. She sensed the girl was secretly distressed at the thought of the family parting. They had discussed it before, and all had agreed to accept separation if it advanced their earning capacities, especially if they remained in contact with each other.

Lucy suggested a walk into the city. Cynthia declared she would stay with Avalyn, begin packing, and make sure the cottage was in order before they slept that night.

I told my cousins that we must take hold of every opportunity, Lucy told herself scornfully, as she walked with Tage, Yolanda, and Jaybee to the city. *But what did I do with that young man's offer of marriage?* She shrugged her feeling of loss away, thinking, *He was just out to taunt and tease me. prince, indeed!* She shivered at the thought of Ludwig, wondering again why there was such a difference between the two men.

Maybe it's because Ludwig gave me the coin, she pondered. *It was a bribe; of course it was a bribe. But, why did he want the widow to report secretly to him? Why would Ludwig want to find Lucy?*

Puppet shows, and yet more puppet shows. At Lucy's prompting, Jaybee painstakingly counted seven different stalls, using all the fingers on her right hand and two on Lucy's, her left thumb never leaving her mouth. As each show required a penny to watch, they did not linger long, but moved from one to the next.

Candy-carts and cake stalls beckoned. Tage and Yolanda wanted to loiter here and watch candies being made right on the stall. Tage declared, "Look! There are a dozen different types of candy and hundreds of cakes."

Vegetable stalls displayed every vegetable they knew, and more. Meat stalls, where one could choose a live animal and have it butchered right there on the wooden block.

Lucy went to a vegetable stall and purchased onions and cloves of garlic. She diligently chose a freshly cooked rabbit from those displayed on a meat stall, secured it with a penny, and told the vendor she would return later to collect it. She then gave Tage and Yolanda three pennies each and told them, "If we are separated, you must come back here and I will meet you. Come before the sun begins to sink too low in the sky."

Sure enough, Lucy later found herself separated from Yolanda and Tage. Jaybee clung to her arm and both stared in wonder at the clamor and busyness going on about them. Purchasing a hot buttered corn cake for Jaybee, Lucy also bought four large red apples. Remembering the two at home, she added an apple for each, and a crusty round loaf of fresh pumpkinseed bread.

Sitting on a bench-seat in a grassy rectangle east of the square, both Jaybee and Lucy became fascinated by the large numbers of sparrows and pigeons flitting, hopping, chirping, cooing, and begging for a crumb or two. Jaybee had eaten both apple and core, but Lucy broke her core in two and threw it to the waiting beaks. They laughed as the birds flocked about the scraps, jostling and dueling one another until finally one piece disappeared and a pigeon flew off with the other, followed by many hopeful competitors. The remaining birds hopped closer, eyeing Jaybee and Lucy, expecting more charity.

"The prince! The prince!" This cry broke Lucy's peace as though someone had declared war. She stood in great concern as the news circulated among the crowds of people in the marketplace and square. "The prince! The prince! Prince Lothar is coming!"

Horses' hooves sounded out on the wide paved road circumnavigating the huge square. The cry grew more intense. "The *prince*! His Highness! His *Highness*! The *prince*!"

People rushed, forming lines on both sides of the street, and Lucy found herself moving involuntarily with the throng. Jaybee was at her side and Lucy entwined the small fingers in her own. Jostled until she was near the front line, Lucy stared as the procession came closer. Hating the feel of bodies close to her, she elbowed those nearest, seeking to gain some space, but there was no escape. People pressed closer still.

"*The prince! Hurrah! Hurrah! Long live the prince! Long live Prince Lothar!*"

Lucy heard her heart pounding in a strange manner. Now she would discover the truth. Was the handsome young man at the pool really the prince? In a moment she would know.

Lucy recognized the uniforms worn by the cavalry and footmen: red and gold, with a touch of blue. Then Prince Lothar rode by, wearing a golden crown and riding a white horse.

It was the prince! Slightly behind him rode a young man. *Ludwig,* Lucy heard the name sound clearly in her mind. She held her breath as Prince Lothar looked her way. His eyes seemed to look through hers, just for a breath, and then he waved to the crowds.

He did not see me any more than he truly saw anyone else. Lucy smiled. *It was him! And he didn't know me. But why did he say such things to me? How strange. Or did I just dream it?*

As people began to disperse and return to their various pastimes, Lucy felt relieved, yet disappointed. Feelings of loss mingled with a deep sense of emptiness. Her grip tightened on Jaybee's little hand as they turned back to the marketplace.

Tage and Yolanda were waiting when Lucy collected their rabbit. Lucy paid the man and as she turned to Tage, he grasped her arm. "Come with me," he commanded, moving off.

Not fully recovered from the press of the crowd, or from viewing Prince Lothar at close range, Lucy obeyed wordlessly.

Leading her across the square, Tage turned to Jaybee and Yolanda, commanding, "Wait here. I want Winnie to see something."

Tage stopped in front of a large notice board.

"What is it?" Lucy demanded, and then saw her name written on the board. She read the large bold words of the notice in a thin whisper.

INFORMATION REQUIRED

Leading to the whereabouts of the maiden named LUCY:
Aged 17-20 years, blue eyes, blond hair.
Also the whereabouts of an old hump-backed widow-woman who knows of the maiden Lucy. Both seen between Passcau and Nisa.
Give information to Sir Marten, Chief Brigadier:
Armies of Lotharingia.

Large reward for proof of whereabouts.
WARNING:
Penalties exacted for deception upon those who misinform.

Lucy turned and looked around the square with great concern. She felt the whole world was staring at her in accusation. To her surprise, people carried on their business, taking no notice of the young widow-woman. Her eyes met the solemn, steely stare in Tage's probing gray-blue eyes. "Lucy...widow with the hump!" he hissed. "But why? What have you done?"

Lucy's heart thumped at the warning she read in his teasing tone. Striding across to the girls, Lucy ordered, "Walk on ahead." She turned and spoke to Yolanda, pointing, commanding, "Go! Walk! The road to the cottage. I need to talk with Tage. Walk on, go!"

When the girls were some yards ahead, Lucy told Tage about her encounter with the prince at the pool. She played down Lothar's words and tainted the story slightly. However, Tage knew enough of his cousin to realize her bent against men and her fear of a marriage like that of her parents.

"I should report you," Tage finally declared in the silence as they walked. "I should go to that Chief Brigadier." He laughed and teased, saying, "I wonder how much it would be worth?"

Lucy retorted, "You're all the same...you're growing up into one of them. I was hoping you would be different, Tage."

Tage snatched her hand, gripping it affectionately, saying, "Oh Winnie...Lucy. You judge men because of your fear, but we're not all the same. It's only because of Cher; the raid...and your bitterness...how can you keep hiding yourself? You are much too beautiful to hide beneath those hideous masks and make-up. I'd be doing you a favor. Imagine! Lucretia Melville, presented to the king and the prince, at the palace, and..."

Lucy fiercely shook him off her hand. She interrupted his daydream, speaking loudly, "Tage Melville. You know that's impossible! More likely I'd be thrown in prison. How dare you suggest you would tell on me!"

Shaking his head, Tage laughed, "If Prince Lothar *did* marry you, then someday I'd be first cousin of the queen of Lotharingia. How much closer to royalty could one be?"

"And as queen, I'd see you hanged!" Lucy retorted. She stomped ahead of him and he strove painfully to catch up. Turning, she appealed, "*Would* you go to them? Tage?"

He did not answer, but smiled.

She halted her walk and took his hands. "Please, Tage. I must know if you'd tell them?"

Tage was silent as he tried to comprehend the fear lying behind Lucy's words. *She'd run away, that's what she'd do,* Tage thought, hoping he was wrong.

"I can't believe that...that the prince would put up a notice about me," Lucy said, shaking her head. "And I can't believe, Tage, that you'd report me!"

"And I can't believe that you'd turn down such a husband," Tage contended, heating up to his argument. "You say you care about us all...you want the best for us; yet you'd pass up such an opportunity. Think, Winnie-Lucy, what it would mean. None of us would ever be hungry again. You must give up your ridiculous fears, Lucy. I don't believe you'd be caused to suffer due to your father's wrongs." He drew a deep breath, asking, "Did...did the prince say...did he say that...that he loved you?"

"And what if he did? He couldn't mean such words. Love just doesn't happen like that. What do you know about love, Tage?"

"More than you do, obviously, Winnie," Tage responded, trying with all his might to walk in time with his cousin. He said softly, "Mother and Father truly loved each other. They told me that they fell in love at first sight, even before either said one word to the other. Mother told me once that when two people fall in love, it's as though a key opens the door to a beautiful new existence of giving and receiving love. It's like that, too, when we accept God's love. I hope you find that key to love, Lucy."

With great effort, Tage increased his uneven step. "I know you don't let me talk of their faith and how much God loves us, Winnie...Lucy..." Grasping her hand to slow her pace, he said, "You need someone to love you. You do! I just wish and pray.... How do you know the prince is not that love, that special one who God wants in your life?"

Lucy stopped walking and turned to glare at Tage. "Tage Melville, if you ever tell on me, I'll never forgive you. You know nothing of love, to entertain even one thought of betraying me!" She turned and stormed away from him, almost running, catching up with the two girls who carried the purchases.

Tage hobbled along behind them, hating his lameness. With each lop-sided step he took, he muttered, "Bitter...bitter...bitter...she's so bitter..." Biting his lip at the pain in his leg and knee, he slowed his gait, knowing he could not catch her again. He mused, *And I've forgotten to pray for her. Oh, Lord, forgive me. Lucy needs You, God! How else can she learn about love?* He whispered aloud, "Mother and Father knew love for each other and they both loved God as well. I want to be like them when I grow up."

Before Tage arrived at the cottage, he had inwardly pledged he would pray for his cousin every day. He sensed her fears were greater than before and, with the passing of time, she was becoming more negative and embittered.

The evening atmosphere was strange. Each of the six in the cottage behaved as though the others had a contagious disease and this was their last evening together.

Cynthia retired early, declaring they must all rise early. They had devoured every seed and crumb of the bread and licked the bones of the rabbit completely clean, making Lucy wish she had bought a cake or a fruit loaf. *It would have helped the atmosphere of melancholy that surrounds us tonight,* she mused. Aloud, and in her most positive tone, she said, "We'll do as Sinclair demands. Cynthia, Yolanda, and Tage will live in the Grand House as servants, and I will take Avalyn and Jaybee with me to seek out other accommodation and work. Luck has been on our side before..."

"Not luck, Lucy. Not luck!" Tage interrupted.

Her mouth dropped at this, Tage's second challenge to her that day.

He added nothing further, but turned away and moved off to the bedchamber he would occupy for this second and last night. His emotions were jumbled. He cared much for Lucy and Cynthia and his sisters. He loved them dearly. The separation from Lucy and his two youngest sisters would be hard for him. But the thought of the Grand House, with its opportunities! He would be living in surroundings similar to those he remembered with great joy of his home in Cher. He wondered what the servants' quarters were like.

Ignoring the calls of "Goodnight, Tage," he closed the door. He would pray, and somehow he might find sense in the coming separation.

"Not luck," he whispered as he blew out the candle and knelt to pray.

Tage felt as though the world's problems sat on his shoulders.

"I'm not strong enough, Lord, to bear this heavy burden. Please take it, Lord, and bear it for me. Oh Lord, Lucy must not trust in luck. Please help her find that key that will unlock her heart to love. She needs your love, Lord, your true, eternal love. And Lord, she needs the love of a good man, one who loves you too."

Chapter Five

Lucy decided to take the donkey and cart with her until she found accommodation and work, then she would sell the creature. With the cart, the donkey should fetch a good sum. But first, she would use them to take the chest containing Cynthia's and Yolanda's possessions to the Grand House, with the small chest containing a few keepsakes for Avalyn and Jaybee.

With Tage's help, she loaded the furniture and mattresses back on the cart. When Tage, Yolanda, and Cynthia were settled, Lucy intended to return with her two younger cousins and collect her trunk, now hidden in the bushes near the cottage. For a reason she could not explain to herself, Lucy did not tell Tage or Cynthia where she had hidden the trunk.

To their surprise, Sinclair himself greeted them at the servants' entrance. When he saw the cart, he ordered two footmen to take charge of it.

"Come in, come in." Sinclair's tone and manner were most patronizing. When the six were over the threshold and moving toward the office door, he said, "Follow Neville there, the Master himself awaits you. He has some questions."

Spinning around at these words, Lucy found her forearm firmly gripped by Sinclair's strong, relentless fingers. She gasped at the closeness of his large uniformed frame and would have followed her first instinct to fight and escape, but she saw a footman close on Sinclair's heels and knew there was nowhere to move but along that corridor.

Why do I feel so afraid? she asked herself, trying to shake Sinclair's unwelcome grip off her arm. *Perhaps...because I had not expected to meet the Master. Lord Tullus.* Projecting her voice up a decibel, she spoke firmly, "Do you mind, Sinclair! You're hurting my arm!" She heaved an over-stressed sigh and shuddered when his grip slackened, but he still held her arm.

Propelled to a large, elaborate chamber, Lucy finally shook Sinclair off. The footman knocked, opened the door and announced, "Widow Winifred, Mistress Cynthia, and their charges, Your Grace." The aristocratic man sitting at the desk stood.

Speaking to Lucy, Sinclair bowed again, introducing, "Lord Tullus, the master of Tullus Hall."

Simultaneously, Lucy and Cynthia curtsied, followed by the girls, whilst Tage bowed. They were overawed at the close sight of a real live lord. No one spoke. Lucy felt her heart beating in her throat, the pounding of it preventing her from swallowing. She was sure she would choke.

Lord Tullus frowned disdainfully as his gaze wandered over Cynthia's shabby costume, before staring at Lucy's outfit. His beady scrutiny drifted finally to rest on Lucy's blue eyes. "Widow Winifred?"

"Yes, Your Lordship," Lucy answered, lowering her eyes.

"You're the late Lord Melville's widow?" Lord Tullus asked, his tone making Lucy jump. He was speaking of her father and she could not find the voice to express the lie she had been living.

Gathering her wits, she asked, "You knew him?"

Instead of answering, Lord Tullus indicated the children, saying, "These are your late brother-in-law's children?" When she did not answer, he asked, "And Cynthia was...is...their nurse?"

Frowning, Lucy grimaced and queried, "May I ask, Your Grace, why you are questioning us?"

Lord Tullus sat and opened a thick book. "I will ask a question of you, Madam, Lady Melville. Why is it that you're traveling the country-side like penniless vagrants seeking shelter and employment?"

Without realizing it, Lucy sank to sit on the plush sofa, the girls copying her. Cynthia plunked herself down in a velvet-covered chair, wringing her hands in worry.

Relieved that his questioning was not about her disguise, Lucy answered in a weak tone, purposely sounding tired, "What else could we do, Lord Tullus?"

Frowning, the Master of Tullus Hall swept his eyes along the row, then rested them upon Tage. "You are Tage Melville, the only male Melville heir left alive."

His eyes went back to the book on the desk and he continued, "You were all reported as missing, presumed dead. Indeed, it's believed you are all deceased." Looking back at Tage, he said, "If you truly are Tage Melville, and I have no reason to doubt it, then you are Lord of Melville Hall in Cher, and..."

But Tage interrupted, "We have no wish to live in Cher!"

"I've not finished, young man. There was a considerable inheritance left by Lady Melville, your...ah...aunt...here and her late husband. It included the castle here near Verdun and other estates and..."

He smiled suddenly and the action lit his countenance, but there seemed something calculated and knowing about his grin. Looking directly at Lucy, he said, "If you are indeed Lord Melville's widow, you are extremely wealthy, Madam."

"But...but..." Lucy stammered, confused and feeling vulnerable to be forced to speak of her father. "It...it...I believe...it...was all...confiscated. My...my...my...h-husband, he died in sh-shame..." Lucy almost added "wearing the uniform of our enemies" but she could not form the words on her trembling lips. Unbidden tears sprang to her eyes and she dropped her head into her hands.

Lord Tullus stood, saying, "I'm sorry that it grieves you to speak of your husband, Madam, but you obviously did not hear the good news. Lord Melville was buried with great honor here in Verdun. He was enshrined in a specially commissioned sepulcher, right beside the royal mausoleum. He was not working for the enemy, but *against* them, at the orders of our King Lothar."

Lucy's mind reeled, unable to take in the news that her father was not considered a traitor, but a hero.

Lord Tullus pursed his thin lips, and then continued, "You'll remember, Madam, the king had great affection for you. He almost married you, didn't he? He'll certainly be most interested in the fact that you're not dead. I feel certain that he'll send for you when I report the good news, which I must do without delay, today. Now, tell me, you had a daughter, Lucretia. What..."

But Lucy stood, gazing at Tage with fear-stricken eyes. The lad stared back, and Lucy knew he expected her to reveal her identity. Without a word, she pivoted and darted for the door, dragging it open, moving swiftly out into the corridor, seeking to escape from her impossible lie.

"No. Please." Lord Tullus strode quickly around his desk, following Lucy. He called to the footmen, "Stop her! Be gentle. You must prevent her leaving here." Turning back, he questioned Cynthia, who, with the children, was right behind him. "What is wrong? Why does such good news make her so unhappy? Why is she so frightened?"

Cynthia clicked her tongue, following him along the corridor. She decided not to give Lucy away. It was up to the girl to reveal her identity when she was ready. She said, "That raid, it were dreadful, it were. All our minds were turned for some months."

But if Lord Tullus heard, he did not pause. Lucy opened the outer door where she fought feverishly with two footmen who sought to restrain her without harm.

Struggling and twisting, Lucy kicked one man in the shins until he finally immobilized her with two strong arms. This was something Lucy could not endure. Being manhandled in such a manner flooded her mind with dreaded memories, and suddenly she was back in Cher. Lord Tullus approached and her confused mind turned him into the enemy. Screaming hysterically, sensations of terror and fear swamping her, Lucy almost fainted. She lay still, the color of blood bright before her closed eyes and she remembered her mother's murder...

An enemy soldier was holding Lucy from behind, another leering and pulling at her clothes. Within seconds, the man behind was struck in the back by an arrow. He staggered forward, falling on her as he died, pinning her to the ground. The other man was also shot and he slumped down on top of both of them.

Lucy lost consciousness, her vision fading quickly, her eyes closing on the final scene of her own father wearing the uniform of the enemy...

She would not remember who she was for days afterward, but there was one stabbing thought in her mind: she could never, ever trust any man again. How could she when she could not trust her own father, a man who had been so unfaithful to Lotharingia?

"We hid, we did...as you can well imagine, Sir," Cynthia was saying. "The little one was nearly dead for weeks, and what with Master Tage's leg being broke.... Avalyn couldn't wake up, and when she did she couldn't see. And me, well, we can't say that I existed for nigh on six months after...after...and Yolanda, well, she has not spoken since then..."

Cynthia's monotonous voice floated to Lucy's ears. She moaned, wishing she could blot out the description and frightful vision that came with it.

Cynthia was speaking again, "M'lady is comin' round. Sech a shock, and we thought it were all done with. You see, m'lord, we never speak of it...and...Lucy...ah...Winnie...she...she's taken care of us, protected us. Without her, why, we'd all be dead!"

Staring at Lucy lying on the grass outside the house, Lord Tullus could not imagine this widow-woman ever taking care of anyone. She looked too frail even to take care of herself, let alone protect others.

"I'll send to Verdun for a doctor," Lord Tullus spoke apologetically, "and I really must inform the king..."

"Oh, Sir, that'd be like dragging it all up again. M'lady will want to rest and be left alone for a while...she could not endure any...any roy'l con-confrontions." Cynthia clicked her tongue again and repeated, "Sech a shock...sech a dreadful shock..."

The children watched silently as the large footman carried their beloved Lucy indoors. Their serious faces and tear-filled eyes made Lord Tullus aware that they still, indeed, suffered great trauma. He ordered Sinclair to fetch a drink for Lady Melville, and he nodded when Cynthia suggested that a drink of water at room temperature would be best.

"But the Cher raid was over three years ago," he said, looking at Tage who was the only one who seemed unemotional. "Come, lad. Let us talk about it. Surely..."

But Tage interrupted, saying, "It may have been over three years ago, Lord Tullus, but when it's spoken of, it seems like yesterday. If you'd been there, Sir, you would understand what Aunt Winnie is...is suffering. I-I will go with her; she needs comforting."

He followed the procession to the sitting room where Lucy was placed carefully on a sofa. One footman fetched a rug and Tage heard Sinclair say "Fetch Belva."

Lucy lay with her eyes closed, looking frail and pale. Tage turned to Lord Tullus and said, "We've been happy these past two years after we recovered. We've had very little, but we've been together. We'd put the raid behind us. I-I don't think that my-my aunt will take kindly to being reminded of the past. It— everything—was dead and gone, finished."

Tage frowned, knowing he must act the part well for Lucy's sake, or he would not seem very convincing. He wondered how an older woman, such as his mother, would react in this situation. Speaking grimly, and looking up into Lord Tullus' ashen face, he whispered, "This could be the death of her."

Tage realized, by Lord Tullus' dropped jaw, he had finally cracked the man's pomposity. Lord Tullus, with his arm about Tage's shoulder, drew the lad out into the hall.

"Yes," Tage repeated, "this could kill her." He decided to speak while the man was listening and said, "She needs no doctor! What my aunt needs is peace and quiet and just those she knows and loves around her. Not a doctor, Sir, no. She'll just want Cynthia and Yolanda to take care of her. The one thing she can't endure is to have a doctor fussing and questioning. She's frail, as you can see, and sometimes, just sometimes, she becomes nervous...especially in such a situation as caused by your footmen, Sir..."

It galled Tage to lie, but he was well aware that some of what he said was the truth. But, the truth was that Lucy was the strongest, most determined woman he had ever known, yet she had fainted.

He needed time to talk with Lucy, time to discuss and plan with her what they would do next. "If we could only have the cottage, Sir, Lord Tullus, for a few days, I..."

"Not the cottage," Lord Tullus interrupted, his voice now consoling. "She needs more protection than that of the cottage. No, she must stay here. You'll be my guests. I'll have the staff prepare the guest rooms for you. We'll make sure Lady Melville has the utmost peace and quiet. Yes." Hesitating, he then said, "Perhaps...I should send for my wife, Lady Tullus?" Seeing the negative set on Tage's face, he answered for himself, muttering, "No, perhaps a new face would disturb her. But I *do* have to inform the king, lad. Your Aunt Winifred is of high note in our kingdom."

Again his hand moved around Tage's shoulder, and he said, "Later, when you have some time, I'd like to discuss the battle at Cher with you. The records speak of Lord Melville and Lady Winifred's daughter, ah, yes, Lucretia, your cousin. There was no proof Lucretia died at Cher. Perhaps..."

Tage shook him from his shoulder and began backing away, his eyes wide with anxiety. "I don't wish to speak of the...of...Cher! No, Sir, Lord Tullus, please excuse me." Turning, he fled to the sitting room, hoping to speak with Lucy. He felt hot and bothered. *I don't want to be the one to tell him. It's not fair. I hate to lie. I must speak with Lucy. She'll have to tell him, she'll just have to...*

Chapter Six

Tage whispered in Cynthia's ear, "When that woman Belva comes, keep her away. I must speak to Winnie, and we need to be alone." Taking the glass of water from the footman's extended hand, Tage spoke softly, "Drink this, Aunt Winnie, it will help revive you." He was well aware that her faint may have been because they had not eaten breakfast, as there had been no food. Lucy had expected some bread and rabbit meat to be left for an early morning snack. Tage smiled; they had all overeaten last night, as if it were their last meal ever. Eating had replaced the usual family chatter.

Belva arrived bearing a small silver tray laden with dainty cakes and tartlets. Speaking in her authoritative upper-servant tone, she announced, "These are for her ladyship. There's a tray for the rest of you in the parlor, if you please. I've been told that Lady Melville must have peace and quiet." With that, she nodded to the footmen, who herded the girls from the room.

Bending, Belva spoke in Cynthia's ear, saying, "You'll agree with Lord Tullus, Mistress Cynthia. He's sent a messenger into Verdun for a doctor."

Hearing this whispered message, Tage's eyes met Lucy's and he knew she heard. "Eat something," he hissed, tendering the tray, speaking softly in her ear. "We'll think of something, if we can get rid of our audience." His eyes met hers and he knew she trusted he was seeking to help her.

Both Cynthia and Tage refused to leave the sitting room, and Belva finally ceased demanding their exit. Submitting to Tage's request for "Peace and quiet for my aunt," the footmen also left the room. Tage heaved a sigh of relief to see the three now had no eavesdroppers.

"I have no idea what we should do," Tage confessed to Lucy, and then he added, "I just want you to know, Winnie...Lucy, that I love you very much and, after all you've done for us, I want to help you to be happy." He saw tears welling in her eyes, and wondered at her maudlin display of sentiment. Lucy rarely shed tears; she was the bravest, the optimist, the one who always wanted to believe the good, not the bad.

"I...to think...Father..." Her blue eyes, though sequined with teardrops, were bright with pride. "He...he was loyal. Oh, Tage! Do you not realize what this means? If only...if only I had known." Lucy was quiet, thinking of the prince. She had felt ashamed, unworthy. She had accepted her father's crimes as a stain on her name forever, but now, it could be different.

"I prayed for you last night. I fell asleep praying on my knees, Lucy. I asked God to show you that He cares for you and He loves you. I-I'm sure he is answering that prayer." Tage wanted to say much more, but he knew from experience that he must tread lightly. Then, he thought bitterly, *But I lied today! I lied for her.* "I need time...it's hard to think here..."

"I'm sure you need to think, Winnie...Lucy!" Tage said, rubbing back and forth across his forehead with his fingers, fearful himself about what would happen next.

Cynthia, forgetting that 'Winnie' had originally been her idea, spoke, "I just wish you could stop all this pretencing! It'd be best all around if you could jest be y'self, Lucretia Melville. I could abide it if you told them, but I think none of us will rest easy if they find you out and *us* for being your helpers to keep you from getting known."

Clicking her tongue, she then added, "To think of it. Yes, I do perchance remember that King Lothar were interested in your mother. It were when she were even younger than you, about sixteen, she were. And yes, I do remember that it were voiced, when she stayed in Verdun...she and the king..."

Cynthia, realizing she was repeating gossip that Lucy would not have heard, nor understood, changed mid-sentence, saying, "Fancy Lord Tullus is going to tell His Majesty..."

"I heard what Lord Tullus said, Cynthia," Lucy sighed. "I feel quite ill about the whole affair. It's obvious that I can't meet the king, not as Winifred. And...and I don't know what to do about...Lucy. We—that is, I, I should have stayed in Passcau..."

"No!" Tage contended, adding firmly, "I believe that everything will come right when you make up your mind, Lucy, to be yourself." He looked into Lucy's eyes as he spoke.

She looked away and he urged, "Think about it, Lucy. Cynthia is right. You should be yourself. There's no need for disguises, hiding under hideous masks, or wearing widow's weeds. Not to talk of our lies. Cher is over, Lucy, gone, finished. You heard what Lord Tullus said. It's time to be yourself." In his discerning gaze, he calculated her stubbornness and knew Lucy was not ready to be herself, yet.

As though to put Lucy to the test, a knock resounded on the door. Lucy pulled the blanket up over her, saying, "I'm sleeping. Tell them not to disturb me."

Belva entered, saying, "I've been ordered to report how Lady Melville is faring." Glancing at the inanimate form, the closed eyes and pale face, she whispered, "You should loosen her bonnet and remove the cloak. I expect the doctor to be here within the hour." She sniffed as though wondering why Cynthia had not already done these things.

After Belva left the room, Tage sprang to his feet and softly closed the door. Sitting close to Lucy again, he said, "She's gone, you can open your eyes." He grinned at her affectionately. Raising his eyebrows, he asked, "So, what are we to do next?"

Lucy threw the rug off and stepped to the window where she pulled the thick drape across, then carefully peered about the grounds. "I need time to think. I'm glad I hid my trunk near the cottage."

Again inspecting the grounds, she declared, "I'm going to leave, but I won't go far. Look, it'll be easy for me to climb from this window, and as this is the side of the house, I'm sure I can gain cover of those trees there before anyone sees me." Her eyes searched both Tage and Cynthia's faces, and the look was like a farewell caress.

Lucy's voice was dull and sad as she said, "When I've thought the matter through, and carefully considered every option, I might return, or I may keep going. You know I've learned to take care of myself..." Dolefully, she added, "You'll be well taken care of...just...just say...say...not a good-bye, but say to the girls...that I do care, and I will return..."

She could not bring herself to use the word 'love', but her heart said, *I love them all! Dear little Jaybee, kind Yolanda, sweet Avalyn, Cynthia, who is so giving; and Tage, so brave...* Tears slid down her cheeks.

Tage limped to Lucy's side. Grasping her hands, he turned her towards him, saying, "You know where we all are. Lord Tullus will make us stay here. And remember, he'll likely set up a search for you as Widow Winnie. You can contact us here, and don't leave it too long, Lucy, or I'll worry."

He turned towards Cynthia, asking, "We'll promise to keep Winnie's secret as before, won't we?" He knew that Lucy needed this assurance. Cynthia nodded and Tage continued with fervency, "The girls won't let it out, you know that. You have our promise, Lucy, and we'll pray that God will keep you safe."

Looking about the room, he said, "Cynthia can lie down in your place and cover herself with the rug, and I'll try to prevent the doctor from examining her. I'll say you need to sleep and he can see you when you wake. Later, when, and if, they find you're missing, then we'll act as though we don't understand what they're talking about..." He smiled wryly. "We'll make it up as we go along."

Doubt shadowed Lucy's face as she stared at Cynthia. The woman was much taller and bigger-framed than she, but then her hair was the same as the wig Lucy wore. If she lay with her back to the door, covered by the rug.... "Here, Cinnie, exchange bonnets with me. I'll take your cloak so mine can be left folded on the chair there, and your dress is the same color and fabric...as long as they leave you alone to sleep...."

***

No sound of mirth escaped Lucy's lips as she unlocked the trunk with a large key attached by a chain to the narrow leather belt she always wore. The situation was far from funny. It was impossible! But she dared not stop and consider now; she must escape and find a place of safety. Only then could she indulge in the luxury of thinking and planning; maybe then she would see the humorous side to it all. Perhaps Tage and Cynthia were right. Maybe she should throw away all her wigs, masks and disguises and be her true self but she must not make a hasty decision, especially not under the current conditions.

I must keep my mind upon this hour, she warned herself, lifting out a bag containing the most recent disguise she had created, one she had not yet worn. *No one has seen this one!* She was pleased. Not even Tage would know her. *He has never liked my disguises, he's too honest and religious,* Lucy mused, as she changed her clothing in the concealment of the bushes.

The dress she pulled on over her white muslin one was a dull green shade of the style a young maid might wear to market. Over this, she drew a dark green cloak with a hood that lay across the back of her slim shoulders forming a large collar. On her head she positioned a brown wig braided to coil about and forward of her ears in the manner of a very young maiden. The hair was parted in the middle and two shiny-brown 'curtains' hung low on her forehead, changing the cast of her face.

Looking in her tiny mirror, Lucy lightly blackened and thickened her eyebrows, smudging the charcoal for a more natural effect. Using the fine sharpened point of a dark-brown chalk, she moistened it with the tip of her tongue before dotting a few freckles across her small nose. This would be the first time Lucy had disguised herself as a young girl. The other disguises always made her appear older, a widow-woman.

Having folded an old lady's disguise, complete with silver-gray wig, into Cynthia's thick woolen brown cloak, she pushed the bundle into a carry bag. The cloak would make a good rug upon which to sleep. Counting all the coins she owned, she placed them in two separate places: one small moneybag on her belt and the other deep in the carry-bag. Closing her eyes, she listed her meager effects, hoping not to miss some needed article. Drawing out a small sheathed dagger, Lucy placed it on the belt about her waist. Shivering in agitation, she hoped she would never have a reason to use such a weapon. *But*, she told herself, a *sharp knife has many good uses.*

Dragging the locked trunk close to the grassy bank as far under the bushes as possible, Lucy broke a few branches, covered it, then scattered mulched leaves and twigs to hide any telltale marks on the ground. Poking her head out from the bushes, she inspected the area.

A deep, foreign sensation that Lucy deciphered as comforting fell upon her, and her thoughts spoke loudly within her head. *Tage is praying for you. Tage is asking God to help you and to keep you safe. Tage loves you, Lucy. His love is pure, brotherly love.*

Feeling deeply moved and grateful towards her earnest young cousin, Lucy stepped from the concealment of the foliage. Keeping to the bushes and darting between trees, instead of walking directly on the road, Lucy moved cautiously towards the main route leading into the city.

Calculating the time since she had left the Grand House, Lucy was not surprised to see a carriage leaving the city gates just as she approached. It was a closed carriage, but the uniforms of the footmen and the mounted escort were the same livery worn by Lord Tullus' staff. She drew a deep breath as the vehicle turned towards Tullus Hall and she wondered how Tage and Cynthia would cope with the arrival of the doctor. Before long a search would be mounted for the widow Winifred.

Smiling, she told herself optimistically, *You're in control again, Lucy. Everything is fine. Tage is wasting his time praying...God doesn't need to bother about me. I can take care of myself. I'll make haste to the city, purchase food, and find somewhere to spend the next few days, somewhere to think, somewhere safe to hide while I consider what I should do.*

Chapter Seven

Tage sat upright as a knock sounded on the door. He was sure that Cynthia, lying with her back to him, was sound asleep. In fact, he now heard her snoring softly. As Tage opened the door, a footman announced in a monotonous voice, "Doctor Skerry to see Lady Melville."

Tage stepped aside as a massively framed man entered. Close behind was a younger version of the same size and height, and Tage realized that the doctor employed his son as his assistant.

The lad knew he was in the minority as the doctor waved the back of his hand at him, expecting Tage to leave. Moving across to the window, Tage turned to see the doctor removing Lucy's bonnet from Cynthia's head. Prickling all over from the tension, Tage grew wide-eyed as he realized the doctor's misconception.

They think Cinnie is Winnie the widow, Lady Melville. No one is here to say anything else. He watched the doctor counting Cynthia's pulse, whispering to his assistant. They had obviously been warned not to upset the patient. Tage almost smiled. *Who could have imagined such a cover? I thought Belva would come and that she would raise the alarm.*

Sitting up suddenly, Cynthia grasped the rug, obviously upset by the man who peered into her eyes. Before she could utter a word, the large-framed doctor forcefully pushed her back to lie on the couch. He spoke kindly and softly, "I'm Doctor Skerry, and this is my son. We've been commissioned by Lord Tullus to examine you and treat you if necessary. Just relax, Lady Melville."

Cynthia's wide-eyed compliance was eclipsed by the doctor's form, and Tage looked out the window, wondering how Lucy was coping with her bitter freedom. *This is remarkable,* he thought, *Lucy's not going to be missed for a while yet, not if Cinnie can continue the charade.*

The doctor finally spoke, "I'm told you had a faint and that you suffered shock, Lady Melville, but there's nothing to worry about, certainly nothing a few days rest will not mend. Your heartbeat is quite normal, and it's good to see that you're able to sleep."

Unfolding to his full height, he said, "I'll check on you again in a few days. Lord Tullus is concerned, but overly so." Turning, he looked at his son, raising his eyes to the ceiling, and Tage wondered if Lord Tullus often became overly concerned, so much so that the doctor was exasperated with this non-essential visit.

Turning on an artificially soft, sweet tone, Cynthia pleaded, "Please tell them to leave me be. I...I find it so hard to...to meet...strange people...I need peace and quiet...no confrontions..."

If the doctor was surprised by Cynthia's theatrics and mispronunciations, he made no comment.

Opening the door as the doctor approached, Tage stood aside while the two exited. Sending Cynthia a wink, he followed and listened discreetly as the men conferred quietly in the corridor.

"It's typical, Father," the young adult whispered, "Lord Tullus treating a weary old lady as if she were on her last legs."

The doctor frowned, saying, "She certainly shows her age; and she's plumped up a lot. I had the idea that Lady Melville was petite." He turned and frowned at Tage, taking in the features of his handsome face, his sandy-blonde hair and blue eyes.

Lord Tullus himself approached and Tage knew this was the important test. Slipping into the corridor, he closed the door behind him.

Tage asked, "I'd like to know how she really is, please?"

Ignoring the lad, Doctor Skerry addressed Lord Tullus, "You can be assured, Lord Tullus, there's absolutely nothing to fear. The lady is tired and needs rest. She's over-anxious, perhaps a little too nervous, but I'm sure this will pass with a peaceful atmosphere." He paused, and then asked, "Have you positive proof that she is Winifred, the widow of Lord Melville?" To Tage, the doctor's tone held a large amount of disbelief.

Lord Tullus appeared confused for a few seconds before gaining his usual mastery. “We must believe it. I do, Doctor Skerry. You see, she’s not claiming any of the inheritance. She had no idea that her husband was cleared of the charge laid on him for treason. As you know, this was not brought to light until after Cher was regained from the enemy. As I see it, Doctor, she must be Lady Melville, and I truly believe that Tage here is Lord Melville’s nephew; the Melville replication is obvious. I will assist the lad to lay claim to his rights, of course...”

All three stared at Tage, then Lord Tullus offered, “Come and take refreshments before you return to the city, Doctor Skerry, Jeffrey...”
“No, thanks, Lord Tullus. We must return immediately. There’s rumor that our king is ill. I was requested to be ready in case another opinion was required but you know how the king is, he’d be breathing his last before he called a doctor.”

“That’s not good news, Skerry. Do keep me informed. I trust it’s not as you say, with the king.” Lord Tullus led the way along the corridor.

Doctor Skerry turned to his son, who hissed in his ear, “The king is far more ill than that woman in there, Father. I wish Tullus would not call us out like this, but then, when we heard the name *Melville* we’d have come anyway, wouldn’t we?”

Looking past his son, the doctor said, “Take care of your aunt, lad. After a day’s rest, a short walk in the fresh air would serve her well.”

Reentering the sitting room, Tage felt both relieved and guilty. He recounted the conversation to Cynthia who was pleased to know she was in such good health. It seemed their pretence would last quite a lot longer, maybe even through the night if Tage demanded that his aunt sleep here undisturbed.

They enjoyed the measure of success that their shared travesty was bringing, but only for Lucy’s sake.

When Belva opened the door, Tage was ready and waiting. Cynthia, covered with the rug, lay with her back to the door as before, and to all observation was asleep. “My aunt would like to see the girls. One by one, of course, and after that, she wants to be left to rest."

Both Tage and Cynthia were eager to know how the girls were faring, whether they had been questioned or felt intimidated. Yolanda entered, happy at first, then she stared about in concern, looking from Tage to Cynthia and back about the chamber. Tage quickly closed the door and explained the situation. He did not over-elaborate, but made sure that Yolanda understood that their cousin needed time away to think and decide her future.

Tage felt proud to recount to Yolanda the news about Lucy's father, over-emphasizing simple mouthed words, so she might feel secure in the knowledge that their hardships were over. Yolanda, being very intelligent, understood and regained her happy mood. She nodded when Tage again commanded, "We must all support Lucy as 'Aunt Winnie' until she decides to reveal her identity."

Avalyn was the one who gave Tage and Cynthia the most information about exactly what was going on out in the main part of the Grand House.

"There are servants everywhere! I could hear dozens doing all sorts of little tasks that we would normally do ourselves. And, I heard things that I wasn't supposed to hear, just like always. I already heard that Winnie is in good health, and that Uncle was loyal and not a traitor. They're all whispering about it and about us..." Avalyn was cheerful and merry as words tumbled out, describing how they had been waited upon.

"We were introduced to Lord Tullus' daughters. They're very beautiful and wear lovely clothes. I heard one of them whispering about our rags, but really they're not that bad, my dress has embroidery on it. Oh, they're going to find some nice clothes that fit us. I suppose they've grown out of them, and they said we have to wear nightgowns. Maria, that's Lord Tullus' daughter who is my age, she thought I didn't talk, like Yolanda. She was horrified that we sleep in our clothes and, and we are to have baths tonight, hot water with perfume. We had cake and cream, and..."

She paused, and one of the extra instincts Avalyn often revealed unintentionally showed itself as she asked, "Winnie?" There was no reply and she repeated, “Winnie, are you there?” Before there was any reply from either Tage or Cynthia, Avalyn asked plaintively, “Why has she gone? Why is she so afraid of saying who she really is? They all think she’s our aunt.” She burst into tears.

Tage and Cynthia spent a tedious hour with Avalyn, seeking to calm her and explaining why Lucy needed time alone to think. The blind girl did not cheer up, even with the news that her brother Tage owned the title *Lord Melville* and they had a real castle that perhaps they could live in and oversee.

“You’re almost eleven, Avalyn,” Tage spoke severely. “You must grow up. Lucy has been everything to us. Now we’ll have others to take care of us and I’m sure Lucy will come back to us and we’ll be together again. She just needs time.”

He took Avalyn’s hand in his and, with the fingers of his other hand, he gently touched her lips, saying, “We must be true to Lucy and let her be the one to tell the world that she is not our aunt but our cousin.”

Tage went on to explain about the prince who thought he would like to court Lucy, how he had seen her in the woods, also that the king had once considered marrying Lucy’s mother.

“The king’s wife, Queen Matilda, died about nine years ago. The king would be in the position to remarry and evidently he would remember Lucy’s mother and wish to meet her, expecting of course that she’s a widow. So, you see, Avalyn, whomever Lucy chooses to be, she feels threatened.”

Avalyn suddenly saw the humorous side of the scenario, and she burst into bubbly laughter. Tage and Cynthia both joined the merriment and when they had expended their pent-up feelings laughing at their dilemma, they felt much better.

Avalyn reached for Tage’s hand again and said, “Let’s all pray together and ask that Lucy just be herself, as God made her. I’m sure that’s what...Mother and Father...would want her to do, and we can pretend that they’re here with us, sharing our prayer.”

Jaybee had to be treated differently from the other sisters. Tage told her little about Lucy's reasons for leaving them just now, but majored on the benefits of being here, in the Grand House. Jaybee could cope with one day at a time only. She was much more immature than Yolanda or Avalyn had been at the age of six. Jaybee was only three when the raid occurred. Lucy and Cynthia were the only mothers she could remember. Lucy had been the one who comforted her in the trauma and pain of having been stabbed. It was Lucy who had rescued her from beneath a heap of dead servants.

Jaybee snuggled close to Cynthia now, sucking her thumb and closing her eyes. Tage knew that this was prelude to Jaybee being introverted and uncommunicative.

He shrugged, knowing that Jaybee's frame of mind would suit the situation well. However, before she returned to be with the other girls, he warned her, "Jaybee, I want you to listen." She did not open her eyes and he continued, knowing she was really listening. "We must keep thinking that Winnie is our aunt. We must keep pretending there's no person such as Lucy, just for a day or two. Even if you are asked about a cousin called Lucretia, you must pretend that she is Winnie, just like we always have. When Winnie comes back to us..."

He paused, knowing that statement was about another day, in the unknown future. He did not finish it, but said, "We're going to stay here, live here, and have lots to eat, and nice clothes to wear. Winnie will share it with us when she comes, but we'll all just have to enjoy it for her now. You know she wants us to be happy, don't you?"

Opening her vivid blue eyes, Jaybee jumped off Cynthia's knee, pulled her thumb out, and exclaimed, "Katie is only a year older than me, and she is the youngest, just like me. She said when I get back from here she's going to show me her dolls. She said she has *fifteen* dolls! She's going to give me one, Tage, and she told me that I can ride her pony tomorrow."

Both Tage and Cynthia wore relieved expressions when Jaybee ran from the room, gleefully taking hold of a footman's hand to go and see Miss Katie and the dolls.

For Tage, the night was extremely long. He lay across the unlocked door of the sitting room whilst Cynthia slept on the couch. Having partaken of a sumptuous five-course meal in this very room, he was uncomfortably full. He had paced, wishing he could walk outside in the grounds, but when Belva came to check on Lady Melville, he blocked her from entering the room, whispering that she was sleeping but very lightly and she must not be awakened. He was thankful that Belva did not ask about Cynthia.

By midnight, Tage had decided he would end this portion of the continuing drama and at last there would be some respite for him and Cynthia. He tried to remember what it was like to sleep in that four-poster bed at the cottage, but the hard floor, not much softened by the rug, caused the memory to evade him. Feeling guilty for the lies he had told and been party to, he knew he must pray for Lucy. Before falling asleep, he confessed his lies, one by one, and prayed that he might have strength not to tell any more. *I'm not like Lucy, I'm like Father and Mother; they didn't tell lies, and I know Avalyn hates lies. Please, Lord, help me to be truthful.* Then, as Tage tried to fathom a way to tell the truth without revealing Lucy's secret, he almost despaired. *What a tangle. I'll be glad when it is all over and Lucy can be Lucy.* With this thought, he fell into a fitful sleep.

As the sun rose to waken the sleepy sky with golden light, Tage told Cynthia of his plan to act quite normal, to say that Winnie had left the room; at least this was the truth.

"Let Lord Tullus and his servants and footmen discover that she's not on his property. They'll take a while to search, and then we'll agree with them that Winnie has not been herself and it just might be possible that she headed back towards Passcau or somewhere like that. I'll offer to help look for her. That way, I might be able to meet her in the city."

He wondered what his cousin would look like, sure that she would not be dressed as an old widow! Tage watched the sky brighten, again praying for his atypical cousin.

It was a prayer that Lucy felt as she opened her eyes to find she was lying where she had fallen asleep, on the marble floor of her father's tomb.

Chapter Eight

The young, girlish maiden, threading her way through the stalls of the marketplace, was as insignificant as the vendors and buyers. The only ones interested in her were those who wished to advertise and sell their wares to her. She shook her head at combs and ribbons, cheap necklaces and chunky rings, bread, candies, and cakes. She halted, however, at a bench where an old man was molding candles. He left his melted mass when he realized she was a genuine buyer.

Choosing a thick candle contained in a handy wooden holder, Lucy remembered something else back in the trunk, and she inquired where she might purchase a lighter. Directed to another stall, she received a full demonstration on the workings of the various types of tinderboxes. The man in charge of this business took no notice as Lucy attempted to tell him that she already knew how to use one. Finally, to gain his attention, Lucy stepped away. Within seconds, she was the owner of a small tinderbox, similar to the one left behind.

One place was paramount in Lucy's mind: her father's tomb. Lord Tullus had said it was alongside the royal sepulcher. There was no sign of any tomb near the square or marketplace, and Lucy decided to inquire.

"Please, kind lady, would you tell me where the royal mausoleum is, and how I may get there?" Lucy asked a woman selling corn cakes, having just purchased a hot one. It was dripping with melted butter, and Lucy licked her fingers hungrily.

The woman replied, "Just beyond the palace. It's down the hill, the walls are by the northern city walls." She pointed as she spoke. Lucy did not want to express her ignorance about not knowing where the palace was, so she nodded and moved off.

Feeling anonymous and unthreatened, able to hold her head up and walk without stooping or pretending, was almost as delicious a sensation as feeling young. After devouring the corn cake, Lucy bought a small bag of fruit before leaving the market place and walking in the direction the woman had indicated.

The palace dwarfed every building nearby, and as she approached, Lucy was overawed at the majestic towering edifice of gleaming marble tiles, tall pillars, graceful arches, and the two minaret towers crowned with golden spires. High pikes on the fence surrounding the building were tipped with gold, against which the scarlet, white, and gold livery of the guards was resplendent in the dazzling sunshine.

Pausing to ask a passing washerwoman the way to the royal mausoleum, Lucy started as a mounted company rode towards the palace gates. Scarcely comprehending the woman's reply, Lucy scrutinized the row of riders to see if the prince was among them. The men did not look her way and she breathed a sigh of relief when the gates closed behind the following foot soldiers.

The palace glistened in the afternoon sun as Lucy circumnavigated the guarded palisade, moving on the far side of the paved road towards the downward gradient leading to the mausoleum. It was much further than she expected and Lucy grew weary. She longed to draw out the flask of sweet cider and quench her thirst, but realized this would be most unacceptable, especially by a young maiden walking unescorted along the street.

She realized being unaccompanied was most improper. She paused just long enough to pull off her cloak and roll it into a bundle to carry under her arm. The bag had not seemed heavy before, but now it felt like a load of bricks.

A small crowd surrounded the royal mausoleum and Lucy felt fearful, wondering at the gathering. She counted seven carriages lined up along the city wall, their attendants standing to attention. As Lucy watched, she saw ladies and gentlemen with well-dressed children ascending the steps from the mausoleum itself. A man dressed in similar livery as that worn by the palace guards climbed a portable platform and seemed to be waiting for everyone to assemble. From the surrounding walls, small groups of people appeared, obviously discussing the place they had just visited.

The man on the box gained the attention of the crowd by clapping his hands twice. As he spoke, Lucy drew closer.

"Thank you ladies, gentlemen, young ladies, and little gentlemen; thank you for your agreeable company this afternoon. Now that you have seen the wonderful sights and historic places of our beautiful capital city, we ask that you tell your friends and urge them to take this guided tour. Remember, it is once each week, on Fridays, and begins at the eastern gates one hour after noon. Thank you for your patronage."

"You have just joined us," a thin voice said, startling Lucy, and she turned to see a younger, smaller version of the man who had just addressed them. "You'll have to come back next Friday," he said. Patting a large leather purse on his belt, he added proudly, "I collect the fee." As though guessing Lucy's next question, he frowned and, with the posture of a much older man, blatantly surveyed her petite figure from head to toe before he said, "It's five pennies to begin at the gates and three if you join the group in the square. Grown-ups are twice that amount."

Lucy smiled, pleased that he believed her to be so young. "Where...where do you take them...the visitors?" she asked, moving aside as two men carrying a woman in an elaborate chair jostled her. People were being handed into the carriages, whilst others moved away on foot.

"Come next Friday and see," the lad taunted haughtily, and moved away.

"Do...do you go to...in...the palace?" Lucy asked.

"Of course not. But we do all the churches, the museum, the art-gallery, and a few other historic spots. Come and see." His voice was mocking, and then he was gone, hurrying to catch the orator, bounding down the few steps to the mausoleum.

Lucy hurried after the boy and as they reached the doors, she begged, "Please, I'd like to have a look." She could see that the passage on the other side of the doors descended steeply into darkness.

The older man turned and stared in surprise, "Sorry, miss, but we lock up now. At sunset, the king's guards come and guard the place till morning. It's not a good idea for a young lass to go down there on her own. Come back next Friday." He turned away and continued with his task of locking the heavy gilt doors.

Beckoning her aside, the boy whispered, "You can see into the royal mausoleum if you go around the back and down into the adjoining tomb, but it will be dark, we extinguished the torches..." Regretting his words, he said, "Better that you come back next Friday..."

Knowing he expected her to agree, Lucy said, "I'll see if I can..."

Without looking back, the lad hurried to gain step with his superior, marching behind the man, away from the mausoleum and up the steep paved road.

Lucy moved along the wall base. Seeing the area now clear of people, she followed the scent of lavender, moving around the mausoleum. Under a tangle of climbing roses was a stone archway. A stone stairwell moved down, down. Lucy soon found the way dark and uninviting. Still the steps led downwards, until she felt she would lose her footing and the steep passageway would swallow her. The perfume of lavender, roses, and jasmine lingered even in these depths.

Pausing, Lucy loosened the tie on her bag and drew out the candle and holder with the tinderbox. Lighting the wick, she proceeded, feeling much better in the comfort of light during this unfamiliar trek. She had not imagined the tomb to be so deep, and relief flooded her when she discovered there was no door blocking her entrance, just a low narrow archway leading into a small marble-lined chamber. Wondering how she would be able to see the royal mausoleum from in here, Lucy extended the candle and moved around the central oblong monument.

A heavy metal gate was set in the opposite wall and, when Lucy held the candle close to the lock, she saw there was no handle and that the only means of entry would be with a large key. Without thinking, she set her bag on the floor, placed the candle beside it, and fumbled for the trunk key on her belt. To her amazement, the key fit, and there was a heavy grating sound as she turned it. But when she pushed on the gate, it did not move. Twisting the key again and shaking the gate simultaneously, brought the desired results. With a feeling of unreality, Lucy stepped through the opening, taking the key with her, and leaving the gate slightly ajar. Fascinating epitaphs filled the royal mausoleum. Lucy read of princes and princesses who had died, some at birth, others just a few months old. Lucy read the poetic epitaphs on two tiny marble coffins set into the wall and discovered that Prince Lothar had two sisters. What a massive place! Royal people had been enshrined here for more than a hundred years.

Lucy found the tomb of Lothar's mother, and was deeply touched when she read the wordy eulogy and descriptive epitaph. Tears seeped down her cheeks as she remembered that there was no such place for her mother. *My mother was buried in a mass grave at Cher, nameless and unknown; as were Aunt Phoebe, Uncle Tage, and my baby cousin Terry. And people must have believed we were buried there too.*

Surging over her like a warm wave of sunlight, the wonder of the tomb she'd just come through filled her being. *That must be Father's tomb. They laid him as close to royalty as possible...no one else was granted such an honor!*

Lucy hurried back to the small sepulcher. Her fingers wandered over the marble effigy, so cold and hard, atop the marble coffin. She re-read the epitaph and walked around her father's likeness until she lost track of time. Some time later, she drank from the flask and, realizing she was exhausted, locked the gate, curled up on the floor, and fell asleep.

Morning dawned before she opened her eyes again.

Stretching in the darkness, Lucy could think of no other place she would rather be. *This frigid chamber of death and abandonment is so very precious,* she thought. *Here I find hope and fulfillment and respite from all my fears. I'm sure this tomb is the very place I can find myself, and obtain the courage I need to be myself.*

She smiled and whispered, "Oh happy place of death! What strange twist of destiny brings joy from the grave? I can hardly believe that such contentment can rise with joy, from the bowels of the earth. Such good news as this brings me consolation beside the grave of my dearly beloved father." Throwing herself across the marble statue, Lucy said, “Oh, Father, I pray you can hear me. I beg you to forgive me for doubting you. May you be in a happy rest.”

Lucy was glad her father’s remains were not openly displayed here, as in some tombs. He was encased in the great marble coffin upon which lay the precious carved marble replica. Worked in intricate detail, the reposed figure, with hands clasped as in prayer, wore the Lotharingian battle dress, and a carved marble sword lay at his side.

Tage is praying for me. This returning thought made Lucy frown. *I’m barren of his faith, and my heart is as cold and lonely as this tomb.* She searched her mind to recall some of the teaching given in the Grand House where her aunt and uncle had lived; when she sat with her cousins listening to the chaplain telling stories about the Bible and the Son of God.

Lucy remembered a story, which had made her shudder. The chaplain had told of Mary Magdalene, who, with two other women, had gone to Jesus’ tomb, taking with them embalming spices that they might anoint the dead body of the Lord Jesus. Jesus’ body had been laid in the sepulcher, but, three days later, when the women arrived, he had disappeared; The Son had risen. Death and the grave had been conquered!

I know how Mary felt. Lucy could scarcely contain the welling up within her heart. *This tomb here is empty of shame and misery, just as the tomb was empty of the body of Mary’s Savior. I feel it speaking to me...of victory and honor.*

Lucy stood and prayed aloud in the dimness, “Oh, please, God, help me find the faith that Mary had, the faith that Aunt Phoebe and Uncle Tage had, and that Tage now has. Thank you that Tage loves me enough to pray for me...” Taking up the thick candle, she drew it closer to the tomb.

Holding the flickering flame near the marble face, Lucy again marveled at the likeness. Kneeling, she reread the words engraved on the side of the tomb. They were now etched into her memory, but it thrilled her to read them aloud, “*Here rests the Earthly Remains of Lord Terence Edmond Melville. Loved Husband of*

Lady Winifred Melville, Beloved Father of Lucretia. All taken at Cher. Loved, Faithful Servant and Dear Friend of King Lothar III. He Died that Others Might Live. He Gloried in Serving his Country against many Perils. He was True to the End.

"True to the end. He died that others might live. He died that others might live," Lucy whispered, then read the epitaph again. She wanted to encase the words within her mind, to bask in the reality of her father's bravery and loyalty, to understand this was not a hopeless dream, but a triumphant victory.

I still find it difficult to grasp, our name does not carry the dreadful stigma I believed. Tage can hold his head up, and say, 'I'm a Melville!' The girls will be able to find worthy husbands. And I...?

Lucy pulled a bread roll from her bag and devoured it hungrily. Deeply contented, she puffed out the candle flame and curled up, pulling the warm cloak around her. Sleep, peaceful sleep! The sleep she had experienced last night. Sleep so very sweet, for the first time in over three years!

Imagining herself at the pond, she visualized the prince, standing close to her, so close she could almost touch him.

Prince Lothar. Lothar Charles, the prince of Lotharingia. We are friends and I have nothing to fear when I tell him my name. Lucretia Melville, daughter of the *Lord Terence Melville.*

No, the prince will not spit at the sound of my father's name...

Chapter Nine

Muffled *rumble*...then another...*rumble*... Shuffling footsteps echoed strangely in the depths of the mausoleum. Lucy roused.

More shuffling footsteps, a little unsteady.

The sleeping maiden became lucid.

Clutching her cloak and the bag she had pillowed her head upon, Lucy groped for the dead candle, snatching it off her father's tomb.

Thumping heartbeats sounded in her ears as the shuffle became louder and louder. Someone was approaching. She tried to swallow, but her throat would not respond and she felt she would choke. Crawling around to the far end of her father's tomb, Lucy braced herself for the coming confrontation.

Ghosts do not shuffle...I don't believe in ghosts...it's not a ghost... A blazing flame illuminated the small space. With incredible relief, Lucy realized the light was on the other side of the gate. The invasion was happening in the royal mausoleum. Holding her breath, Lucy wondered why the glow was steadier; but dared not look or she may be detected. Slow footsteps resumed, unsteady, shuffling, and Lucy wondered at someone visiting the mausoleum alone.

Perhaps a night watchman? No, it's still day...maybe midday, or early afternoon. Who then would come to this tomb? She wondered if the invader had descended from the street, but could not remember hearing the heavy doors being unlocked, only that strange rumbling noise.

Heavy breathing possessed the mausoleum now, and Lucy wondered if the visitor had fallen asleep. No. The shuffling footsteps resumed and Lucy listened as they almost faded from her hearing. Slowly, laboriously, they returned, then all was still, but the heavy breathing continued.

Lucy was frozen, unable to move.

Time passed painfully, and she wondered what had happened to the shuffling person.

Footsteps. Steady, definite footsteps, more than one pair. These boots' owners had a purpose to fulfill. Lucy, imagining soldiers—*many* soldiers—cowered behind her father's grave, wondering why she had stayed here. Her eyes widened as flickering orange light brightened the dimness. She started at the sound of Prince Lothar's deep voice.

"Father! Father. You should not have walked that distance, and certainly not alone. We should have commissioned a carriage. Rolt, send for one now!" There was the sound of retreating footsteps.
A tired voice commanded, "Leave us, Ludwig, Weber. We wish to speak with our son alone."

Lucy started again at the familiar name and her remembrance of Ludwig.

High and husky, a voice protested, "But Sire, please. You..."

"Leave us, Weber, I'm here with my father. Olaf and Lars will help us when we wish to ascend. Close the passage."

As reluctant footsteps moved away, the rumble came again, and Lucy wondered how many people still occupied the chamber.

As silence permeated the mausoleum, Lucy gingerly wriggled her way towards the gate, wondering what she would see, if anything. *Floor level will be the safest,* she told herself, and cautiously slid her cheek along the marble floor until she could see into the royal mausoleum.

Wriggling a little further along, she saw two men, some distance away. They were near the step-passage, wore the scarlet livery of the guards, and stood at attention, on guard.

Closer to Queen Matilda's grave, Lucy saw two more men, one supporting the other. Prince Lothar was the taller and from where Lucy lay, she could see him in profile.

An older man, wearing a jeweled crown, leaned heavily upon the prince as though seeking both support and comfort. With trembling fingers, the older man reached out and touched the brow of his wife's statue.

An age seemed to pass, and Lucy, stiff and cold, shivered inwardly. Prince Lothar's deep voice, though soft, cut the silence, making Lucy start. "Father, please. You must come away and rest."

"We shall, my son, we shall. But we fear for you." The old man looked up into his son's face, "We fear for Lotharingia. It is the first time we've not felt at home in our own palace." He looked around the chamber and then turned to view the two guards. Very softly, he murmured, "It's the first time in this life that we have felt so...so very fearful; already we feel traitors treading upon our grave..."

"You are anxious for naught, Father. No traitors shall tread on our graves, but if they do, we shall not be here to be troubled about it."
"Son...Son. Have you no feelings for Lotharingia?"

Lothar emitted a contrived laugh, obviously trying to make light of his father's disquiet. "Yes, but its intrigues bore me, and I find little to delight in, Father. When I'm your age, I shall think of a brighter kingdom where all will be beautiful, like an everlasting forest of tall green trees and sparkling waterfalls. You, Father, by the years' statistics, are nearer than I to seeing Mother again, yet you do not feel the wonderment that you should..."

The king was silent.

"It will be many years, Father, before you join our ancestors in this place."

"Son, for you to be right would mean you could read the future. We only know that we have this hour, together. For a...a few days...now..." the King's voice broke. A long silence followed, and Lucy drew back as the king turned and looked across at the gate. "Come aside, Son, come aside." Leaning heavily on Lothar, he guided the way to the gate where he grasped hold of it for support.

"It is the pain...and it...catches...my...breath...away..."

The gate rattled loudly, then ceased as the king leaned his back upon it. Lucy lay prostrate, striving not to breathe. She bit her bottom lip hard enough to draw blood and hoped fervently she was not caught in this eavesdropping position.

"I wanted...to speak...alone...with you, Son," the king whispered. "It...has been...impossible...and we gave up the idea. This...is the only place...I thought of...where we could find...privacy to think...to consider..." The gate rattled lightly with his labored breathing.

"We...*I* have reason to believe that we cannot trust those closest to us." The king gasped at the exertion required to state a complete sentence in one breath.

"Why, Father!" Lothar exclaimed, then whispered, "Who do you speak of?"

The king's gasps became violent, causing Lucy to draw further away from the gate until she was behind her father's tomb. The gate now rattled loudly.

"Father? Father! Can you hear me? Father?" Prince Lothar said, his deep voice strained. "Olaf! Lars! Help us! Quickly!"

Running boots reverberated in the mausoleum.

"He collapsed! Olaf, take one side, help me carry him back to the palace. Weber can tend him there. Bring a light, Lars."

Lucy listened as the footsteps slowly moved away from the chamber, their flickering torches creating eerie shadows all around. She waited, feeling breathless and panicky. The rumble returned, turning Lucy's fears to curiosity, and she longed to know where the rumble came from. The footsteps resumed, followed by another rumble. Then, all was quiet, except for the pounding from her heart.

Unwilling to move far, Lucy wrapped the cloak around her trembling body. The fear she experienced had spoiled her haven and her peace of mind.

Is there nowhere I can go to think? Not even here. The king is wrong! There's no such thing as privacy. He couldn't speak to his son without those two guards. He's very troubled...and ill. Prince Lothar didn't seem concerned about his father's fears, but he was upset with his father's failing health.

Rocking herself back and forth until she was calmer, Lucy lay with her head on her carry-bag. *I mustn't return to the outer world, not for an hour or more. A carriage is going to be sent here for the king, and he won't be here. I hope they don't come down here. When will it be safe to go out into the world? Who else knows about the passage between the mausoleum and the palace?* Closing her eyes, and picturing the welcome nature of the little cottage on Lord Tullus' estate, Lucy began to reassure herself. *Why should I be afraid? They are not looking for a young maid. I'm safe here...* She fell into a light slumber.

Waking refreshed, Lucy wondered about the time of day. Ravenously hungry, she ate the remaining piece of fruit and the last bread roll. She needed more food. Wondering why she had not purchased more, Lucy lit her candle, checked that her wig was straight and well secured, retouched her make-up, and then packed everything back into the carry-bag. *I'll sleep here another night,* she decided. *I'll leave the carry bag and dagger here, but take some money and the key.*

Extending the candlelight high, Lucy investigated every nook and cranny of the small tomb. It was perfectly built, and obviously not ancient like the royal mausoleum. There were no hiding places, no hole where she could stash her bag.

With a forceful shake and twist, the plied key again unlocked the heavy gate, and Lucy took her belongings, with the candle, into the huge crypt. The massive area, broken up by numerous graves and shrines, had many ideal hiding places. She decided to investigate more when she returned. *Perhaps I'll discover the opening that caused the rumble. But, perhaps, it's not for me to know. It's none of your business, Lucretia Melville.* But the idea gave her a feeling of superiority. She knew something about which the average Lotharingian girl had no idea. The king had a secret passageway between his palace and the mausoleum!

Reaching to feel behind the tiny form of a marble babe, Lucy was pleased there was space enough to conceal both the candle and the bag. She shuddered involuntarily as she imagined the sorrow of laying a tiny baby to rest in this lonely mausoleum.

Locking the gate, and ascending from her father's tomb, Lucy was surprised to see the shadows lengthening and deepening; it was late afternoon. In spite of her anxiety regarding the King's visit to the crypt, Lucy felt rejuvenated and full of energy and life, optimistic and young. *This is what it feels like to believe in one's parentage, to feel worthwhile,* she told herself as she ascended the road towards the palace.

The marketplace was dismantled, and it upset Lucy to discover most food-stalls were either sold out or closed down for the day.

"Come in the mornin', Dearie. Early. Ev'rythin's fresh then," A woman told her, selling her two spotted apples at a discounted price.

Lucy purchased a few cloves of garlic from the same woman, and then wondered why. She had eaten garlic in the past to make herself obnoxious, and the ploy had worked. Most men, indeed, most people, kept well back from her after one sniff. But she had not eaten any for some days, now. Her last lot had been left with Cynthia who liked a little now and then, and the best way for Lucy to be accepted by the family, they had discovered, was for all to eat a little.

Apples and garlic. Lucy devoured both apples and all the garlic as she moved back in the direction of her chosen abode, realizing even as she walked, that retiring shades of orange were radiating from the sinking sun as it signed its last signature by turning the day into a crimson twilight.

The fear and trepidation of the previous hour returned as Lucy descended the steep street towards the mausoleum, wondering if she could sleep there again. Perhaps she should collect her bag and return to the Grand House.

What shall I do? What shall I do? she pondered.

The guards the lad had spoken of were taking up their positions, and Lucy sighed in frustration to see more than a dozen scarlet uniforms spaced around the area. The passage to her father's tomb was blocked. *What do they guard against?* she asked herself. *Maybe they think someone will break in and steal a statue, or are they afraid of someone damaging the mausoleum? Perhaps they think someone might try to enter that passage leading to the palace...* While Lucy mused on an answer, she crept to the wall beside the road, staring in dismay down at the guards, wondering where to go.

I'll have to go back to the cottage. But I hate to leave my bag in the mausoleum...

Hearing the sound of deep voices over the wall behind her, Lucy flattened herself against the stone structure, hoping the dark shadow would conceal her if someone were to look her way. Double gates, a few yards up the hill, squealed open. Wondering if this was a residence, Lucy realized she had nowhere to go. She could not go up the street, nor could she descend. It was a violation of honorable conduct for a maiden to be on the streets after sunset without an adult chaperon. Lucy fervently wished she had worn the widow-disguise. Few people took any notice of a wandering old woman. Here she was, looking like her young cousin, Yolanda, caught in this ludicrous impasse.

Maybe, she thought, *if I run, I can pass the gate before anyone exits; if I linger, they'll surely see me.* Lucy snatched her skirt in one hand and, clutching her green cloak in the other, fled up the rise, crossing to the far side of the street.

Her rapid movement, she later realized, was a mistake. Had she slunk along the farther wall, or remained stationery, she may not have been detected. But one guard, with three others, mounting their horses to take up their posts at the eastern gate, saw her; as did a guard at the mausoleum. Immediately, the captain of the brigade sent a squadron to investigate the swiftly fleeing female figure, but they abandoned the chase when they saw the four mounted guards ride out from the casern, a domicile for single soldiers incorporating large stables for their horses.

Lucy ran faster when she heard the sound of hoof-beats close behind. Gaining the brow of the rise, she paused. Lining the straight street ahead she could see the lights from torches. Along the palisade, by every torch, a soldier stood vigilantly on guard. Backing fearfully against the wall, she watched a young soldier spring lithely from his saddle, joined by a companion. The captain and one other guard remained mounted.

"Have you lost your way?" the first man asked, and stepped aside for the other who carried a torch.

Lucy closed her eyes as the two stepped closer. They invaded her personal space. She snatched a trembling breath in terror. This was Lucy's nightmare: uniformed men closing in on her. Gripped in the sensational horror of the past, Lucy flung her cloak at the pair and darted away, running as though to save her life.

The satin lining of the cloak ignited against the soldier's torch, and the sudden, unexpected action caused him to release the flaming mass, tossing it in the air, dancing comically, like a juggling clown, trying to avoid being burned. His companion sprang aside. The fireball rolled under his horse's belly, and the animal whinnied and shied, as did the other horses, as flames hungrily devoured the fabric. Bolting, two horses fled down the street and the other two, prancing sideways and dancing in panic, took the same path as Lucy.

Guards at the nearest end of the palisade stepped out, aghast at the unconventional sight of a fire in the street, scarlet uniforms in disarray, and the sound of terrorized horses. The captain at the mausoleum sent the squadron up the street again, this time commanding them to investigate the matter fully and return with a satisfactory report.

Lucy did not look back, but turned down the first side street, running as fast as her legs would carry her. Horses' hooves and shouts followed her and she pressed herself to the wall to allow the riderless horses to gallop past. She realized that the pursuers had gained the intersection and were now running rapidly along the paved road toward her. Unless she found somewhere to hide, or could become invisible, Lucy feared she would soon be caught. All along this street, gates were secured, doors locked. People would be at their evening meal, or preparing for it.

Lucy slowed at the sight of a group ahead ascending steps into a residence. The people froze, watching the frenzied horses, then turning to view the runners. Lucy swerved down a narrow lane, a passage descending between two residences.

Slipping on oozing sewerage, Lucy was horrified that the squadron was almost on her heels. Stumbling in the darkness before tripping, Lucy shrieked as rough hands grasped her arms, hauling her to stand. The four surrounded her and two riders were close behind. Losing all self-control, and any nerve she had previously, Lucy screamed uncontrollably, continuing with the torturous noise even after the men released her.

The captain dismounted and shouted, "Unhand her!" Not sure the men had heard him, he yelled louder, "Unhand her, I say!" The screaming continued.

One man shouted back, "We're not touching her, Sir, she's deranged!" The screaming almost drowned him out as he repeated, "None of us is touching the maid."

The captain copied the actions of others he had seen in such circumstances. Reaching for the culprit, he grasped her by one arm and slapped her cheek hard. When she did not cease the screams, he shook her fiercely and slapped the other cheek.

Lucy was hoarse by now, and her voice died suddenly at the severity of the unmerciful punishment. Crumpling to the ground, she pleaded, "No! Please, no." Curling up, she covered her head with her arms, whimpering, "Please...go away...go away."

The captain knelt by the quivering mound, asking, "Who are you? Give us your name." He waited and then repeated the questions, adding, "Tell us where you live and we'll take you home."

"Go away...please..." Embarrassment, due to her loss of self-control, swamped Lucy. She knew she was not deranged, she was not back at Cher, she was in Verdun. It seemed this episode, combined with the time spent in the mausoleum, had finally banished the imaginary ghosts that had haunted her, but she struggled to deal with reality. How could she tell these Lotharingian soldiers that they had enacted a nightmare from her tormenting past?

After repeating the questions and receiving the same pitiful answer, the exasperated captain stood. "We haven't time to waste like this. Take her to the Melville."

Lucy heard the name, and looked up. In the dimness, the captain saw her response. He asked, "Do you live at the Melville?"

Staring in wonder at the repetition of her last name, Lucy did not resist as the captain grasped her arm and hauled her to stand. "I said, do you live at the Melville?"

"The...M-Melville?" Lucy stammered.

"I should have guessed you came from there. Come along, then. We'll take you home." Turning, the captain said, "She's unhinged, best if you fetch a small carriage from the livery-stables."

By this time, Lucy was calm enough to absorb the fact that these uniformed men were not planning to harm her. *Indeed,* she thought, *they...they're...trying to help me...* She suddenly felt very spent and would have fallen had the man not supported her.

"The maid is faint," he stated. Having caught several whiffs of her strong garlic breath, he commanded his subordinate, "Carry her to the livery stable."

Lucy quickly revived at the word 'carry' and as the guard reached for her, she struggled furiously. The captain, not hesitating, slapped her again and shoved her at the young guard who seized her, enveloping her with his strong arms. Bending a little, he prepared to toss her over his shoulder.

"I said carry her!" the captain bellowed, adding, "Like a child, not a sack of grain!"

Chapter Ten

Closing her eyes in submission, yet still frightened, Lucy clutched at the guard's chest sash as though her life depended on it. She wondered if it were the thudding of his heart, or hers, that reverberated in her ears. This was the situation she had always feared; someone would discover her identity and carry her off to prison. Her overpowering nervousness made it difficult for her to view the situation realistically.

A small, closed carriage was commissioned and within this dark vehicle, Lucy managed to gather her wits to sum up her options. "They are not going to hurt me...they are not going to hurt me," Lucy repeated. "Please, God, help them not to harm me." She recalled their conversation. *They're taking me to a place named Melville...it won't be a prison...they would not put a young maid in a prison, surely...*

The carriage moved slowly and Lucy wondered where it was going. *The Melville. What is 'The Melville'?* As the wheels turned, Lucy's composure began returning.

Remembering her disguise, she smoothed and checked the hairpins securing the wig to her own braided hair. Lucy felt for the small velvet bag containing its coins and the key, both attached to the thin tie on her white dress, hidden by the green frock. Sighing in relief that she still had her 'props,' Lucy remembered the burning of her cloak. Picturing the scene again, Lucy began to see humor in the situation, and when the carriage arrived at Melville Castle, she had not only recovered from the ordeal of her capture, but also felt more in control of herself. She decided to continue with the impression that she was half-witted. *Unhinged, that was what the captain claimed.* Lucy smiled. *I'll continue to be unhinged, but I mustn't overdo it. I'll just be moderately unhinged, not fiercely so. I'll pretend I don't understand what anyone is saying.*

A deep voice called, "We have one of your flock here...a young lass."

"You sure, Sir?" a much older voice questioned, and then added, "We're not missing none. We's full up, that's wot. Wot be her name?"

The carriage door opened and Lucy was commanded to step out. Her tardiness caused the young soldier to reach in and, grasping her arm, he hauled her to stand before the man.

Ignoring the question as to her name, Lucy stared, wide-eyed, examining the large castle gatehouse. There was a familiarity about the gatehouse, and then Lucy stared harder at the old man, trying to recall his name. Joshua, or was it Joseph?

"I don't know 'er. She mus' be of the old faith...take 'er roun' the other side..."

Before Lucy could utter a word, she was shoved back into the carriage. The door slammed and the vehicle moved forward. She realized they had entered the castle grounds and the driver was turning the carriage around. Soon they were moving out the way they had entered.

The young soldier again pulled Lucy from the vehicle. Exasperation flowed from his tone as he barked, "I just wish you'd tell us your name!"

"It's Mary," Lucy said simply. She had decided on this name during the journey. This name, stolen from the Mary who had gone to the tomb, was surely a good choice, she thought.

The young watchman at the gates through which the carriage had been driven, stared at her. "Mary?" He stepped closer to Lucy, holding the torch close to her face, his eyes probing the young features. He declared, "Never seen her before. She doesn't belong here!"

The soldier was frustrated. Tapping his temple with his forefinger until the watchman understood the gesture; he then turned and slammed the door of the carriage, commanding the driver, "Take it back to the livery stables." Turning to the watchman, he said, "It's your problem, Tobie. I was ordered to bring her here. We've done our duty." Swinging himself up on his mount, he said, "She was found wandering the streets. Just see it doesn't happen again."

Muttering, the watchman commanded Lucy to follow, but she remained staring at the departing carriage with its mounted escort. Two soldiers had accompanied her, with the driver there were three. Ignoring the watchman, who came to the realization she was not following, Lucy waited until he returned. She shuddered as he grasped her arm. Hating his closeness, she gritted her teeth, determined to follow through with her new charade until she saw an opportunity to escape.

Lucy found herself pushed to sit on a cold stone seat in a vast entrance hall, where the marble floor reflected the few candles flickering in their sconces. She stared in recognition. She had been here, but many years ago. *I must have been little,* she thought. The sound of footsteps caused her to start, but she ignored the approach of the owners. The watchman's footsteps were heavy, but those following were of a softer, quieter nature. *More of a glide,* Lucy thought, dismissing the urge to look. Summoning all of her self-control, Lucy fixed her focus on the flickering flame of a candle.

The night watchman continued on, returning to his responsibility at the gate. The owner of the second pair of feet stopped beside Lucy, waiting, looking, frowning at the maid's preoccupation, yet still patiently waiting. Lucy stood, but instead of acknowledging her confronter, she sidestepped, keeping her fixation upon the candle in the sconce. Moving across to it, she turned; looking back at her own shadow, she frowned deeply as though puzzled.

"Mary. Is that your name?" There was no answer, and the woman muttered, "Pity to waste it on a heathen." Lucy looked at the speaker, who crossed herself and repeated the name, "Mary. Come, child, but don't be too sure we'll have a place for you here."

At Lucy's immobility, the nun circled her, waving the backs of her hands as though herding goats. Lucy did not move, and realized the nun did not want to touch her. Glancing down at her soiled dress, Lucy remembered the sewerage and knew why the woman kept back. The nun's habit was spotlessly clean and the white fabric edging it was starched to a sun-white crispness.

Lucy backed away from the woman. Deciding to humor her, Lucy hurried in the direction indicated. *The castle has been divided in two,* she thought, remembering now her parents' differing faiths. *Father was of the new faith...like Uncle Tage and Aunt Phoebe; but mother, she was of the old faith...oh dear, does that make me a heathen?*

Lucy remembered her mother's visits to the city, and how sometimes she had gone with her, to this very castle. The great hall... Lucy turned at the corner, heading for the place she remembered as cheerful and happy, full of fun and gaiety.

"Not that way. Mary! Stop, come back!"

Lucy, hurrying towards the Great Hall, was surprised to hear voices chanting and as she neared the doors, the sound grew much louder. Pushing the doors inward, Lucy moved inside and allowed the doors to close behind her. She stepped forward, staring in awe at the sight before her. The Great Hall had been redecorated and had lost its former identity: it was now a church. On either side of a long aisle were wooden pews. The front and back pews were filled with nuns, while those in between held a vast assortment of women and children, concentrating on repeating the chanted prayers. Lucy stared in awe at a life-sized Madonna holding a tiny baby. A large golden halo surrounded the statuette's head.

"Mary," the nun opened the doors behind the runaway, and although she whispered the name, many heard, and turned to view the intruder.

The nun crossed herself and curtsied, murmuring, "I'm sorry, Father. Forgive us." The nun grasped Lucy's hand and pulled her from the church. Unresisting for some distance, Lucy frowned as the nun pulled her towards a downward spiraling stone step way.

Snatching her hand away, Lucy shook her head. *That's the way to the dungeons,* she remembered, turning away. "I'm not going down there!" she said, forgetting her identity as Mary. "There are only dungeons down there!"

Tucking her hands into the wide sleeves of her habit, the nun stepped towards Lucy, but for every step she took, Lucy retreated a pace.

"They're not dungeons, Mary, they're sleeping quarters. After a good night's sleep, you'll feel much better." The nun's voice was kind and coaxing.

Lucy tried hard to remember the other side of the castle, where she had been taken first. "I don't belong here," she said, "I should be...on the other side...I'm not of the old faith..."

"Not of the true faith?" the nun corrected Lucy. She clicked her tongue. "Come along, we'll sort it all out in the morning..."

But Lucy was not going to wait to see whether or not there were dungeons or sleeping quarters below. As a small girl, she had been terrified of that particular stairwell, and the gory tales told by servants, stories of torture and confinement. Pivoting on her heel, she sped off along the corridor, trying to remember the way to the other side.

Lucy discovered the corridor she was seeking, and slowed her pace. With a sudden jolt, her heart seemed to stop. A large tapestry depicting the Last Supper hung across her path. Rushing to the obstacle, she pounded on it, but the way was blocked. There was a wooden wall behind the tapestry. Backing away from the dead-end, Lucy wondered how long it would be before the nun came with reinforcements to capture her and throw her in the "sleeping quarters."

What's going on here? Why are children kept in this place? Why is it called The Melville? Remembering the old night watchman, whose name was either Joshua or Joseph...or did they call him Jose? Lucy decided she must somehow make her way to the other side and discover why this castle was divided in two.

The fact that Lucy knew her way about this vast place was invaluable. Whenever she heard footsteps approaching from one direction, she went in the other on a path of suitable escape.

A long, wide corridor had been converted into a dining area, with long narrow tables and skinny wooden benches. Climbing under and over the barriers, Lucy recalled that on this level there were family bedrooms off the corridor, guest-rooms, and a large library. Poorly lit, the corridor was an obstacle course for the girl who could hear someone ascending the steps at the other end.

If the dungeons are sleeping quarters—Lucy felt sure they could not be—*then what do they use the sleeping quarters for?* Lucy was most curious. Stepping into a dark room, Lucy was unable to see a foot ahead. Crouching behind the door she had closed, Lucy waited for the footsteps to pass by. She listened as they began to descend a stairway beyond the dining area. Moving back out into the corridor, Lucy pulled a candle from its sconce and returned to the room.

The room had no beds, but contained tables and benches, similar to the ones in the hall outside. Along the wall were slates, chalks, and books on shelves. The front desk had, among other things, an inkbottle, a quill, and a cane.

"It's a schoolroom," Lucy said softly, jumping at the echo of her voice.

All the old bedchambers were now schoolrooms, and Lucy wondered how many children came here for classes. She estimated each room had places for twelve to fifteen children. *This may be the 'teaching position' that Sinclair mentioned. But then, the nuns do the teaching, don't they?* Lucy stepped out of the chamber and moved to replace the candle in its sconce. As she turned thoughtfully, a man, wearing a priest's costume, stepped in front of her. She stared up at his grave countenance, and suddenly felt very much out of place.

Lucy spun away, intending to weave her way through the tables and benches, but saw that her way was barred. This time, it was the bold young night watchman, aggressively blocking all hope of escape.

"Come," the priest said simply; and Lucy, seeing the night watchman striding towards her, obeyed and followed the priest.

A row of black and white habits with somber faces awaited Lucy as she descended the final stair. Bowing her head, Lucy hurried to keep up with the large black-framed priest who had obviously taken command of the transgressor and her future.

Across the marble reception hall and to the front door, Lucy could feel the very real presence of the night watchman at her heels. He hastened to open the door and to Lucy's surprise, the priest also stepped outside into the cool night air.

"You are from the other side?" he asked, as though to be sure before allowing her to leave.

Lucy felt tongue-tied. It was one thing to lie to the soldiers and the night watchman, but not to this priest, the Pryor, whose name she knew from Cher, one who had been close to her mother. Her blue eyes filled with tears and she stared at the blurred stones beneath her feet.

His fingers, very gently, lifted her chin so that her face was turned towards the light of a torch now held by the night watchman. He waited until she looked up at him.

"Is your name Mary?" he asked, and waited for her answer, which finally arrived as a guilty headshake. "Perhaps we should go back inside and talk?"

Lucy's headshake was much stronger. She had lowered her eyes, but now looked back into his. "I do not belong with you here, Sir, but I don't..." She was going to say, *I don't belong with those you would call heretics, either,* but she checked herself. Perhaps it would be better to leave here. This priest would surely discover her identity. She felt certain she would be compelled to tell him the truth. *If I go...perhaps I can escape...but how will I find my way back to the cottage in the dark? I'd rather wait until daylight.*

The night watchman shifted from one foot to the other.

As though he had read her mind in the time-lapse, the priest asked, "Will you promise me that you will not run away, if I allow you to leave here with Tobie?"

Lucy blinked the tears from her lower lids. “I promise,” she said softly. As the priest turned away, she said, “Thank you, Pryor Francis.” She stepped away, following Tobie, but the priest turned back.

Taking a few steps towards the departing maiden, Father Francis watched her as she walked across the courtyard to the gates.

Turning back, he spoke aloud, “How did she know my name? I have not been called ‘Pryor’ since Cher. I must look into this matter further. Perhaps I should take it up with the Padre from the other side. There’s something familiar about that girl’s face and her large blue eyes.”

Chapter Eleven

The walk around the castle walls seemed endless, and Lucy sought a mind-picture of the castle fortress and its exterior walls.

She remembered only one gate. *They must have built another,* she thought. *Perhaps it'll be best for me to stay at this place tonight...I'm so hungry and tired.*

Treading long strides, Tobie had moved ahead; now he stood, staring back at Lucy, watching and listening, as she approached. The torch he held lit up the whites of his eyes and Lucy recognized an expression of sinister greed as he stood blocking the narrow footpath.

"You've some silver on you, girl! Now, will you give it here, or do I take it from you?" Tobie stepped purposefully towards his prey.

Lucy realized the two silver ducats in her moneybag, together with a dozen pennies, had been clinking softly as she walked. She backed away and would have turned to run, but Tobie pulled out a thin, sharp dagger, holding the blade between his thumb and forefinger.

"Run, little girl, and this will end up in your back!" Tobie warned, his uneven teeth barred, causing Lucy to think of a maddened dog. Without taking his eyes off her face, Tobie added, "Then, I will have to throw you over that precipice"—he pointed to her left— "with the others." He stepped towards her.

Lucy stepped up on the stone slab guarding the edge. Tobie paused in his advance.

"I'll jump and take the silver with me!" she threatened, moving closer to the darkness. Her voice was shrill as she spoke quickly, hating herself for her lie, "Or do you think we might come to an arrangement, Tobie?" Lucy wished fervently that she had brought her own dagger; at least she could match his threat. *What a worm,* she thought*, a typical man...*

Tobie slid his foot forward another step.

I must not let him touch me, she thought, and her courage seemed to drain away. *I'd rather jump than have him touch me...*

She called, "Stay where you are or I'll jump!" Lucy felt goose bumps and was certain Tobie planned to use the dagger. She prayed silently, *Oh dear God, please save me from him, and I swear I'll do anything you want!*

"If...if you move back, away from me...back...to the wall...I'll throw you the money-bag." She knew by the way his stance relaxed he would do as she asked. But after that? She shivered, thinking, *He's going to kill me! He planned this before we left the gate. He said 'others.' Others are over the precipice? Dear God, help me.*

"All right, girlie, but don't you try to run off, or..." Tobie, torch in one hand, erect dagger blade in the other, backed slowly to the wall.

Remaining fixed on the enemy, Lucy pulled her outer skirt up, revealing the white muslin and undoing the thong fastening the moneybag to her belt. As Tobie started towards her, she cautioned him, "I'll throw it over the edge..." She was repulsed by the way he ogled her, licking his lips, barring his teeth. She jingled the coins in the bag, bringing his attention back to the sound of silver.

He stood stock still, his eyes on the moneybag as Lucy held it above her head, poised as though to throw it over the cliff. Lucy's eyes were on the flame, and she hoped her aim would be true. Directing the bag at the torch, Lucy scored a hit, sending the torch backwards and catching Tobie by surprise. His thoughts were only for the silver and he lost his command over the dagger. Not prepared for her swift departure, he stamped out the moneybag, snatched it up, and followed her.

Gathering her skirts in one hand, Lucy ran swiftly, trailing her other hand along the wall, hoping she would not stumble over anything in the darkness. She did not pause to listen for pursuit, but continued even when she saw the flare of a torch at the gatehouse. To her relief, the portcullis was raised and the gate open. Light on her feet, she fairly flew under the archway and on across the courtyard, oblivious that both horses and people looked up at her approach.

Lucy did not heed the voices calling, demanding, "Halt! Hey, girl! Halt!" as she raced up the stone steps and across the terrace to a side-door that opened at her touch. With the greedy cunning of Tobie's face spurring her on, and every voice now belonging to him, Lucy's course became automatic as she fled up a narrow stairway. The sound of pursuit was most unwelcome, as were the hands that reached for her at the top of the stairs. Lucy struggled and fought, even when she was flung to the floor and strong hands sought to pin her down. Then a knee was pushed into her back, winding and immobilizing her.

A familiar voice came to her ears. A voice filled with familiar frustration. "Well, well! We have that little mad Mary that I delivered next door!" It was the soldier.

Slowly, the hands released her, and Lucy turned sideways on the floor, doubling up, trying to regain her breath. She closed her eyes, wishing they would go away. *They are not going to hurt me,* she told herself, trying to believe it.

The soldier reached down and hauled her to stand. Knowing now that his presence meant safety against her previous escort, Lucy clutched on to him for support. It dawned on her that all men were not Tobies.

Her large gulps of breath caused her to feel a little faint. She stared around at the unfamiliar faces, hoping to not see Tobie's.

"Oh...I am...safe..." Lucy said. A silence followed and Lucy knew they were waiting for her to explain her sudden arrival. "I...I...I did not...belong...over...there."

The soldier, supporting her, asked, "What are you running from, Mary?" He pushed her from him, frowning down into her troubled eyes, asking, "Why did you run as though you were being pursued?"

"That man! He...the priest...told him to walk me here, and we...we started out...he...he was supposed to...to bring me here, but...he frightened me...he...made me stop...he had a dagger...he was going to...I couldn't let him touch me...he said there were others over the precipice...but..." Lucy paused, wondering whether to mention the moneybag. What young girl would carry two silver ducats? She stared up at the soldier, and was silent; she decided he would not understand.

“What man?” he demanded fiercely, “His name! What’s his name?”

“Tobie, the night-watchman...” Lucy replied. She stepped back as the soldier swiveled on his heel. Two soldiers Lucy had not noticed before followed him, racing down the stairs, bolting along the corridor toward the door. The frightened girl was left with five serious faces staring at her.

A woman elbowed her way forward. Placing ample hands about Lucy’s shoulders, she said, “You’re half frightened to death, and no wonder.” Looking at the others, she said, “Well, don’t stand there gawking! Get back to your places! What kind of welcome is this for a maid in distress?” Clicking her tongue, she said, “Look at your dress, it’s soiled, and you have bruise on your cheek, you’re smudged and dirty, come.” She drew Lucy away, concluding, “The questions can wait till the morning. You look half-starved. We’ll see what’s left in the kitchen for you.”

Lucy found herself sitting at a chunky wooden table in the warmest chamber of the castle, and when the woman brought a bowl of thick soup, the aroma caused Lucy’s mouth to water. The woman broke bread and dropped it into the soup, prattling animatedly, as though chitchat would banish all terror.

“Now, I can’t say as we can find you a bed to sleep in, it’ll be hard enough to get a rug for you, and that’s a fact...” She drew a breath as she looked at the dark rings under Lucy’s eyes, saying, “But then, you look tired enough to sleep anywheres!”

She pushed the soup bowl towards Lucy, “What with that house that burnt down and those chil’ren being left orphans, we had to find beds for seven! Can you imagine? And not one of them poor little chil’ren was over the age of nine! The littlest two with burnt hands, and the oldest had burned his feet...

“Then there were the poor widow wot went missin’—what a to do! And we’re not sure if we’ll get those four chil’ren over at the Grand House; they say there’s one gone missing, but Lord Tullus is just as likely to be taking them all on..." She turned as an older woman entered the chamber, beckoning her.

"Ingrid, you be wanted..."

Lucy, deliberately blocking out all thought of Lord Tullus and her cousins, helped herself to another bowl of soup, having devoured the first; the delicious flavor tempting her to take her fill. The huge cauldron was one quarter full and Lucy did not think they would miss a little more. *How long has it been since I had a hot meal like this?* she wondered as she sipped from the bowl. Her mind was tired and she could not remember how long it was since she had left the Grand House.

The women did not return, and the kitchen chamber was empty of life, except for five fat cats, curled up together on a thick rug by the hearth.

Sitting beside the furry creatures, who purred at Lucy's gentle touch, the girl sat staring into the fire, and after a while she was surprised to find herself thinking about nothing in particular, and most unconcerned about her future. Trying not to think of the past hour, but to consider safety here and now, brought a comfortable feeling of blankness.

With a jolt, she remembered her cry to God. She prayed, "Thank You, God, for saving me from Tobie. It could have all turned out differently." She shuddered and stared at the fire for some minutes, before praying again, "I need to know you better, God, not just to cry help, but how do you speak to me? How do I hear you? Will I ever know what you want me to do?" Her eyelids felt heavy and, yawning loudly, she curled up with her head on her arm, falling fast asleep.

Later, when the soldiers returned bearing the moneybag and enquiring about 'Mary', wishing to question her, they discovered her asleep in the kitchen. Even though they stood right beside her, discussing her and debating whether or not to awaken her, Lucy was oblivious to their presence. She slept until the kitchen staff came before dawn to prepare breakfast for those living in this half of the castle.

Chapter Twelve

Soft voices growing louder disturbed Lucy's dreamless slumber; then the feeling that she was sliding, or floating, turned into a sensation of falling. She was falling over a precipice. As the sense of movement grew more real, she woke.

Springing to a crouch, Lucy nervously summed up her situation. The owners of the four hands dragging the rug and her away from the hearth ignored her. They then lit the fire, preparing for the breakfast cooking.

Lucy relaxed on the rug, hugging her covered knees to her chest, realizing how cool the chamber had become. She watched as the team moved diligently about their duties.

The woman, Ingrid, stood before Lucy, saying, "You'll want to wash, Mary, and I've found a clean dress about your size. The chaplain be wanting to speak with you before breakfast. It'll have to be a quick lick, until later. Come along, then, hurry up, they be waiting for you, and you must'na keep them waiting!"

Later, Lucy, thankful that Ingrid left her alone for the 'quick lick,' pulled the plain brown dress over her white muslin. Hanging in gathers from under her armpits, the dress made her look very young. Ingrid returned and Lucy followed the bustling woman along the corridor to the door of a room Lucy recognized as the parlor.

Knocking on the door, Ingrid opened it, announcing, "I've brought the maid Mary." She curtsied and turned to Lucy who had followed her, shyly dropping a curtsy also. Backing up, Ingrid spoke proudly, in an introductory tone, "Our Chaplain, Brother Daniel." Her eyes flicked towards the priest as she added, "And...Father Francis..."

Lucy's bright blue eyes were not upon the two men of the cloth, but busily scanning the room, which was plainly, yet sparsely, furnished and her mouth dropped open in surprise. All the valuable tapestries that had graced the walls were gone. Instead, the parlor room was lined with bookshelves holding large volumes. The plush furniture had been replaced with a few wooden stools, and the corner where the large sofa once stood was occupied by a wide desk, behind which sat the chaplain. Father Francis stood beside the desk.

Lucy now realized Ingrid had left the room, and she was alone with these two awesome, but innocuous, holy men.

The chaplain, Brother Daniel stood. "You've been here before, Mary, some years ago?" To him, the answer was obvious, written in her concentrated recognition and puzzlement.

Lucy did not answer. Instead, she turned her attention to the chaplain, staring into his face, unable to bring words to her lips. She took a step backwards. The priest, as though thinking she was going to abscond, stepped swiftly and grabbed her hand as she backed further away.

Father Francis gazed deeply into Lucy's eyes, and Lucy found it difficult to look away. "Tell us about yourself," he commanded, drawing her to sit beside him on a stool. "Tell us the truth; is your name, Mary?"

Lucy looked at the man behind the desk, and she knew it was he who wished to question her. Turning back to the priest, and twisting her hands nervously in her lap, she replied, "No, not Mary, I...I just used that name..." She looked down at her hands, forcing herself to hold them still.

"Then what *is* your name, and from where did you come?" the chaplain asked, a note of impatience in his voice. At her silence, he asked, "Do you have parents or a guardian?"

Lucy shook her head, wondering how she would be able to avoid the truth, and trying to determine whether or not it mattered any more. *Can't I just tell them my real name...and take off this wig? Perhaps the moment of revelation is here...*

Before Lucy could speak, a knock sounded on the door as it opened. Standing before the chaplain, a young soldier bowed first to Brother Daniel, then to Father Francis, before turning back to the chaplain, who stood and moved around to Lucy.

"We wish you to tell us exactly what happened last night, from the time you left Father Francis, until you arrived here," the chaplain stated. Frowning, he added, "Do you always tell lies?"

Lucy looked at him, and with a sudden memory, she smiled, showing two deep dimples. "Most of the time, Brother Daniel."

"You know me?" he asked, his frown deepening the contours of his face. "Your frankness perplexes me, Mary. I don't know you, do I?" He stared down into her eyes, then glanced at the priest.

Lucy looked from one to the other, saying, "I know both of you. You see, my father was of one faith. And my mother was of the other faith. As for me...it was very confusing. It still is. They are both dead, and I wonder where their souls went? How do I know which one to follow? Is it the old faith or the new faith?"

"The core of our faiths is the same," the chaplain began.

"The new is a continuation of the old," the priest said, smiling.

"You are friends?" she asked, confused.

"As God is One," the chaplain said, then asked, "You have something to tell us about your parents?"

Lucy would have revealed that her father was Lord Melville, the castle's namesake, but the soldier impatiently interrupted: "Please, Chaplain, we need some facts, we need to know. Tobie..."

The priest interjected, speaking earnestly to Lucy, "We'll speak of other matters later. For now, you must tell us the truth, Mary, you see..."

Brother Daniel spoke up, "Tell us exactly what happened last night, Mary!"

Lucy looked from one to the other, wondering why it was so important that she tell them about Tobie. In halting tones, she recalled the foot journey—leaving out the jingling coins—and stammered a little at the confrontation with the dagger-wielding Tobie.

Listening intently until the girl told how she escaped when Tobie was distracted, the soldier shook his head. "You left something out!" he exclaimed.

"Have you told us everything?" the priest asked.

"Yes. No," Lucy said. "I..." She shrugged and sighed, saying, "I...I used to work. I'm not as young as I look..." She saw contempt on the soldier's face. "I do embroidery," she asserted, then added, "It's not just ordinary embroidery, and...and I have savings." Tilting her chin, she indicated the priest's elaborate garments and said, "One is paid handsomely for the needlework on your costume, Pryor Francis."

Knowing the men wanted her to speak of last night, she continued, "Tobie heard my two silver ducats and a dozen pennies clinking in my moneybag. He was filled with greed..." Lucy remembered his sun-tanned, oily face, the torch shining on his wet lips. Grimacing at the chaplain, she said, "It was not just greed for the money. I am chaste, but I know he wanted more than my moneybag..." Her eyes sequined with tears that she blinked away as she said, "I...I don't pray very much, but I asked God to save me from him, and He did..."

Lucy went on to explain how she had thrown the moneybag at the flame, putting Tobie off-balance. "I ran, and I did not look back."

Brother Daniel moved back around his desk and drew the blackened moneybag from a drawer. Opening it, he placed the two ducats side by side and made a stack of the twelve pennies. "Is this yours?" he asked, his eyes searching her face.

"Yes, it's mine." She looked up at the soldier, asking, "Then...you found it on Tobie?"

"Yes, we found it on him," the soldier said, his voice grim. He turned to the chaplain. "We need Mary as a witness." Looking back at her, he asked, "You're not unhinged, then? You faked your hysteria?"

Lucy grimaced, then answered, "I... Well, no. Some of it...I..." She bowed her head and the three leaned toward her as she murmured, "I was at Cher, three years ago; the raid...it made me afraid of...men in uniforms. Although I was not really harmed, other than emotionally, I cannot bear anyone," she glanced up at the soldier, "anyone...like you...near me. Your uniform is very similar to the enemy's." She shivered.

Silence followed Lucy's statements, and the men exchanged glances. The soldier, having the information he sought, moved first, snatching up the money and bag. "My commanding officer will want this as evidence. We'll have the man, Tobie, transferred for interrogation. Mary will be safe here. I'll let you know when the trial is fixed." He bowed and quickly left the room.

"Trial?" Lucy asked, confused.

The priest took Lucy's hands in his, drawing her around to face him. He spoke softly, carefully choosing his words, "Over the past six months, there have been eight young maidens murdered, their bodies discovered below the precipice where Tobie accosted you. All had been stabbed: two in the back, while the others had stab wounds all over." He saw the horror on Lucy's face and his grip tightened, preventing her from pulling away.

"To our shame, we never suspected Tobie. He always had a good alibi...until last night. Leo, with two other soldiers, caught Tobie before he reached our gates. He was breathless because he was running when he heard the men's pursuing footsteps. He must have followed you, hoping to prevent you entering...then he returned the way he had come."

"I—I thought he was just boasting. There really were...others?" Lucy felt sick. "*Eight* others?" Their grim faces were affirmation enough, and Lucy drew a deep breath, realizing how close she'd come to death. "I would have been the ninth..." she whispered, then thought of the murderer and shivered. "Where...where is...Tobie now?"

"He has been locked away, but is to be taken somewhere more secure." The priest released Lucy's hands and stood, "I must go and make sure they take him without any fuss..." He turned and spoke to the chaplain, "I'd like to continue this conversation, Daniel."

"We will, Francis. Let me know when you can come, and we'll have Mary join us here," the chaplain said, as he shook the man's outstretched hand.

Before anyone could move, the door was knocked upon and flung open. A young man entered. He stared at Lucy, then turned to the desk, saying, "There's news from the palace..." He waited.
Brother Daniel spoke to Lucy, "Breakfast will be served in a few minutes. Shall we still call you Mary?"

Lucy glanced from him to the young man, and said to the chaplain, "I want to tell you my story, Brother Daniel, but it would take some time, and the moment is not right..." Stepping towards the door, she asked, "Where is the dining hall?" She looked back at the chaplain.

"How long has it been since you were here, Mary?"

"Oh," Lucy's mind calculated quickly, and she answered, "about ten, or perhaps eleven years..."

The chaplain showed surprise as he said, "Then you will go to the ballroom, which is now the dining hall."

"The ballroom?" Lucy's eyebrows shot up in surprise. The glorious ballroom where her mother danced with the aristocratic men of the kingdom; leaving her father in Cher because he believed dancing to be a sin; the ballroom where Lucy was permitted only during the day, but she longed to see at night, when the beautiful ladies danced with the handsome men until dawn. Lucy wondered how her mother would feel about the ballroom being turned into a dining hall, and used by people of the new religion.

One thing about it, Lucy mused, *Father would be delighted!*

To the chaplain's surprise, Lucy laughed lightly before leaving the room. Closing the door ever so carefully, she caught the beginning of the young man's announcement, "The king is dying, and he is..." But the light click of the door brought the thick wood between them, preventing her from hearing more.

Lucy watched as children of all ages and shapes and sizes entered the dining hall. One thing was common: their clothing, like Lucy's, was made of plain brown fabric and completely unadorned. The atmosphere was somber as the children took their places, standing at the tables. Older people, obviously the overseers, stood behind a long front table.

The large chamber displayed no sign of having been danced in; indeed, it was plainly an eating room. Rows of narrow tables, wooden benches on either side, stretched across the marble floor.

After a painfully long silence, broken only by coughs and yawns, Brother Daniel entered and took his place beside a young sober-looking woman. "We will pray and return thanks to our Heavenly Father for the mercies He provides," the chaplain announced, staring about the room as children everywhere bowed their head and closed their eyes. Looking directly at Lucy, he said, "For those who are new, we bow our heads and close our eyes when we pray..." Then began the long, wordy prayer.

Had the chaplain not looked directly at Lucy, she would have glanced around, but due to his scrutiny, she dared not. Her thoughts wandered while he gave thanks for their safe night's rest, followed by praise for the blessings of good health. She listened as he prayed for the children who had been rescued from the fire, thanking God that their burns were not too severe. He then uttered names of those in authority, praying for them, asking God to bless and keep their benefactor, the king, in his moment of grave need, and to impart strength and comfort to Prince Lothar. As he prayed for those who cared for the king, naming many names, Lucy's mind wandered.

When the *amen* rang out, echoed by all, Lucy was thinking of Tage and her cousins, wondering how they were faring.

Brother Daniel's voice pulled Lucy's mind back to the dining hall. "We have twelve new children with us today. The children of the Latham household, and the children of Claude. They will come forward as I call their names. Charles, William, Peter, Caroline, Sarah, Megan, Emery, Kathryn, Demas, Paul, Christine...and Mary."

Lucy watched in fascination as a boy with bandaged feet stepped out, carrying a small toddler whose hands were also bound. A small girl, with one foot bandaged and the other bare, carried a baby whose arms and hands were bandaged. Other small children, all shy and nervous, followed.

"Mary!" the chaplain repeated, and Lucy suddenly realized that everyone waited on her.

Blushing deeply, she moved to the front, feeling every eye burning upon her. Like a turning ocean wave, all in the room bowed their heads. The chaplain prayed for the newcomers, and Lucy blushed again when he prayed for the orphan 'Mary', thanking God for her safety. He ended with a prayer for the provision of food for the day and for its application to the well being of their frail bodies.

Ushered to a side door, Lucy found a bowl of thick oatmeal thrust into her hands. Commanded, "Take a spoon," Lucy obeyed and was then directed along the corridor, through another door, and back into the dining hall. Table by table, the children moved silently, yet eagerly, to collect their portions. Lucy turned her attention to the oatmeal, which she found to be delicious.

Next, they were each given a piece of bread spread with meat-drippings and Lucy found it tasty also. Food—any food— was wonderful to her palate. Returning to her place with the bread, Lucy noticed that the chaplain's place was vacant, as were several others at the main table, and she wondered where they had gone before the meal was done. Finally, a mug of water was tendered, which like the food was consumed in silence. Several severe-looking women and men paced along the aisles during the meal, as though expecting the children to create a disturbance. The somber atmosphere was contagious, however, and complete docility reigned.

Wondering why it had not dawned upon her before, Lucy realized exactly what the castle was: *It's an orphanage!* She stared around with new interest, thinking, *There are probably children from Cher. I may know some. Then again, it's been over three years, and they would not recognize me like this...*

A bell rang out, causing Lucy to jump.

Exclamations circled the chamber. From the reactions of the older children, Lucy knew the bell toll was unexpected.

Following the throng, Lucy found herself drawn into the large chamber that once had been the castle chapel. It was now a chapel of the New Faith.

The children around her sat on wooden pews and became quiet.

Brother Daniel entered a side door and moved to the platform, standing behind a large pulpit. His head was bowed in prayer for some minutes before he made an announcement that caused Lucy's heart to constrict:

"We have sad news to report. King Lothar is dead. We trust God will bless his son, the new King Lothar of Lotharingia. Let us pray..."

Chapter Thirteen

Father Francis joined with Brother Daniel and together they read Scriptures, prayed for the new king and kingdom, and prayed for religious freedom in which they could worship God as they believed, read the Scriptures for themselves, and teach children about the things of God.

Lucy did not move from the pew after the dismissal. A sense of unreality filled her. Something new, something fantastic was happening in this place.

King Lothar had been of the Old Faith when he was young, but had embraced the New Faith in his latter years. Lucy understood, from the prayers, that they were not sure just where the new king's preference would be, or if he would follow his father and encourage religious freedom. It was known that those closest to the prince were a mixture of both faiths. The fate of the churches was in Prince—King Lothar's hands.

What an awesome responsibility for a young man, Lucy thought, *and while he will be grieving for his father! I hope he has people around him who will give him comfort.*

The chapel was empty now, but Lucy still sat, wondering again how one could know what God really wanted for one's life. *God has so many to think of. One God for all these people. He won't have time for me...*

Lucy moved towards the front. There were no statues or icons, but a simple text above the pulpit attracted Lucy's attention. "Jesus Christ died that we might live."

Moving around the pulpit, she saw the open Bible from which the chaplain and priest had read. She re-read the words: *I exhort therefore, that, first of all, supplications, prayers, intercessions, and giving of thanks, be made for all men; For kings, and for all that are in authority; that we may lead a quiet and peaceable life in all godliness and honesty. For this is good and acceptable in the sight of God our Savior; Who will have all men to be saved, and to come unto the knowledge of the truth. For there is one God, and one mediator between God and men, the man Christ Jesus; Who gave himself a ransom for all. I Timothy, 2:1-6.*

"Who will have all men to be saved," Lucy summarized aloud, "and come to the knowledge of the truth...there is one mediator...Jesus...he gave himself a ransom...for all. For *me*!"

Sinking to sit beneath the pulpit, she rephrased the words, whispering to herself, "God loves you, Lucy...and He sent His Son for you, to ransom you. I can go to Jesus as my mediator. Oh God...you want everyone to be saved from their sins...and how I've sinned!" She closed her lips, afraid to say the words that formed on her tongue...

Lucy the Liar! Lucy the Liar! she heard her conscience accusing her. Turning to see the words over the pulpit again, Lucy murmured, "Jesus Christ died...that you, Lucy, might live..."

Bowing her head, Lucy prayed, "Oh God, I need your help. I'm so mixed up, I hardly know where to begin..." Again her thoughts accused, *Lucy the Liar! Lucy the Liar!*

"Then, I must tell the truth. Lord, help me to be truthful. I'm sure you died for that sin of mine. Please forgive me, Lord...for all the lies..." Two large tears ran down her cheeks as she continued her whispered prayer, "And, God, Father in Heaven, forgive me for all the other sins I've done, for which Jesus had to die so I might live...and help me to live how You want me to. It's so hard for me to do what's right. I need Your help..."

Overwhelming sorrow took her, and she wept and then repeated, "Forgive me, Lord, please forgive me. I'm so sorry..." As a feeling of deep cleansing swamped her, she turned her eyes back to the text. "It's not a religion! It's a person...God's Son, Jesus...knowledge of the Truth, between God and man. It's simply believing and confessing...and being accepted. Thank You God! And please, please help me; help me live for You."

Lucy sat, rethinking the past three years, remembering the struggles, especially in the winter months, to provide for her four cousins and Cynthia. "If only I'd known the truth...about Father...and about Jesus. He died that we might live."

A golden plaque set in the marble floor caught Lucy's attention, and she moved across to read the inscription: "He died that others might live: In memory of Lord Terence Edmund Melville." Her voice was loud in the empty chapel as she repeated, "He died that others might live." She would have knelt, but quick footsteps interrupted her solitude.

"Mary?" The sharp voice was feminine, and Lucy spun around, recognizing the young woman as one who had paced the aisles at breakfast. Two men followed her and she spoke to them in a breathless tone, "It'll be all right...she's safe. I'll take care of her. Go and tell the others we've found her." She continued towards Lucy, and the men left the chapel.

"The words are the same," Lucy said, wishing she could tell this woman about the plaque. She pointed to the text above the pulpit.

"You read Latin?" The woman asked, raising her eyebrows.

"Oh," Lucy said. Then, instead of answering, she murmured, "He was a brave man, Jesus." She indicated the plaque, "And...And...him..."

"He saved my life," the woman said. "Lord Melville told me that God works out everything for the good of his children. There's a purpose in everything, he said, a reason."

Lucy's blue eyes glowed with happiness. "I must remember that. There is a reason for everything. Please tell me more about...about Lord Melville..."

"Sometime I'll tell you about it all, but right now I need your help, Mary. Before worship time, we have to bathe the children who arrived last night. It's customary for everyone to have louse-oil poured on their hair, then we wash it." She stared at Lucy's perfectly set coils, then drew the girl with her, back along the aisle, "The doctor's coming to dress their burns, and we have to bathe them without getting the bandages wet. It's a real mission, it is. By the way, I'm Shalone. I live here and help with the children."

Shalone chatted nervously, all the way to the bath-chamber. Lucy was thinking about her wig, her charade, and how she would end it. She was surprised as people exclaimed, "You found her!" and, "There's Mary! That's a relief!" as she and Shalone walked by. Apparently, they had thought she'd run away.

Lucy longed for the time when her running would end.

Dying embers glowed in the fireplace, and Lucy surmised this was a washroom because of its closeness to the kitchen., making the task of fetching hot water easier. Judging by the number of children now being dried and dressed by several woman, Lucy realized that she'd been duped by Shalone into coming here.

As the children were dressed and led from the room, Shalone and three other women cast their attention upon Lucy.

"It's mandatory for all newcomers to have the oil and a bath," Shalone explained, tightening her grip on Lucy's hand. "Then we have them examined by the doctor. He's coming later. But, for now, come, I'll help you."

Lucy turned to stone, knowing that if these women tried to loosen her hair, they would discover her wig. It was very well made, but close scrutiny would soon reveal that the hair was sewn to strips of scalp-colored fabric.

Bracing herself, Lucy felt a chill creep up her spine as one woman smiled and exclaimed, "Well, it's glad we all are that you're found, Mary. What with that mad murd'rous man having stolen the keys 'n all, we was very worried for you."

"Mad...man?" Lucy asked, staring around at the women who closed in, surrounding her, making her feel nervous. "You...you...don't mean...?" She could not bring herself to verbalize her fears.

"Now, Jess! You've gotten Mary all upset." Shalone clicked her tongue and placed her arm about Lucy's shoulder, saying, "You're safe here, Mary. A company of soldiers is coming to search for him."

"Tobie?" Lucy's voice was incredulous. "They...they didn't take him away? He's loose?" Their sympathetic faces confirmed it. "He...has keys?" Lucy tried to think what keys Tobie would want and why he would want them. "I'm the only witness...alive..." Lucy shook Shalone's arm off her shoulder asking, "Has he got the key to the door between here and...?" Again, the answer was in their faces.

Filled with fear and dread, Lucy would have fled from the chamber, but Shalone and Jess grasped her arms firmly.

"Please Mary, you'll hurt yourself..." Shalone pleaded as Lucy struggled with them.

"Or you'll bruise *me*," Big Jess bellowed as Lucy inadvertently trod on her large toes with her heel. "And I'll not have that!" A fat hand slapped Lucy's face, causing her to crumble to the floor.

Lucy did not cry, but sat perfectly still, gathering the threads of her torn thoughts. *Tobie will be looking for Mary.* Lucy concluded the obvious: *I must change my identity and they mustn't know that Mary and Lucy are the same person, because Tobie will find out, and then he'll be looking for Lucy. He mustn't find me.*

Shaking her head, Lucy looked up at the women staring down at her in concern. She wondered how she could tell them the truth about herself. *I can't,* she told herself, *I just can't! But how can I prevent these women from seeing that I'm wearing a wig?*

A plan formed in her mind as she rose slowly to her feet. "I used to look after several children. I know how to use the oil." Speaking directly to Shalone, she spoke convincingly, saying, "I know how to wash myself, Shalone...please, I don't need to be treated like a baby."

Lucy moved across to the bench table where the flask of oil had been placed. A sandglass stood beside it. "I rub the oil into my hair and scalp, then I turn the glass. While I bathe, the oil will work, then, when the sand is all at the bottom, I soap my hair with this special soap..." She turned and repeated, "Please, I'd like my privacy, it will help me feel better, being on my own, please..." Lowering her long eyelashes, Lucy stared at the floor, waiting submissively a moment before looking up at Big Jess, asking sweetly, "Do you bathe in front of other women, Jess?"

One by one, the women left the chamber, and Lucy was most relieved to see that they left the key on her side of the door. Quickly, she turned it in the lock. There was an instant reaction as the knob twisted back and forth.

"Mary!" It was Shalone's voice. "She's locked the door! Mary!" Shalone slapped the palm of her hand on the door, calling, "Unlock it, Mary! Unlock the door!"

"I said I like my privacy, Shalone, and that's the truth. Just go and do something else for a while," Lucy called, knowing she must act quickly. Humming loudly as she moved, Lucy's fingers reached under the coils, removing hairpins. When the wig was freed from her own plaits, Lucy hesitated briefly before flinging it onto the embers of the fire, knowing as it burst into bright flames, that there was no return. *I'm not Mary and I never again will be Mary. But I wish I wasn't Lucy... I'd rather have my 'Widow Winnie' disguise.* Lucy felt sure that Tobie would not give her old lady outfit a second glance.

To mask the sounds of her actions, Lucy lifted the oil flask and banged it back down on the table, before placing it silently on the floor with the other tabletop items. After studying the two high, narrow openings in the stone chamber, Lucy now worked swiftly, carrying the table and benches to lean against the wall. *I'll keep the brown dress on until I'm away from here; it won't be as noticeable as the white...*

Turning the table top to the wall, Lucy balanced one bench across the legs, and the other at a right angle. It reached almost to the opening's ledge.

Lucy quickly unwound the braids encircling her head and coiled them into a neat oval shape, fixing it at the nape of her neck with the hairpins. *This is how Shalone wears her hair, and she's about twenty-two. I'm sure I'll look older than Mary, now.*

Lucy had second thoughts about her young girl's dress. *They'll be looking for someone in a brown dress,* she told herself, swiftly unbuttoned it, peeling it off, and placing it beneath other garments in a large wash-basket. The white muslin with its delicate embroidery around the calf-length hem was not exactly a street dress, but Lucy knew she would at least look her age.

Mary is gone! Finished, Lucy thought.

As though challenging her, Shalone's voice called, "Mary, Mary?" The door rattled loudly, causing Lucy to jump.

Lucy hastened to the water and splashed it about with her hands, sloshing it over the edge. "What is it, Shalone?" she asked innocently.

"Nothing!" Shalone replied, clearly checking on her.

Climbing up the furniture, Lucy heard the murmur of voices then the clicking sound of a key in the lock. *They've fetched a duplicate key,* she realized, but relaxed when the key her side did not move. *They can't unlock it with the key blocking the lock in this side.* The nervous girl knew they would either have to break the door down, or commission a locksmith to remove the lock.

To Lucy's surprise, the outer wall was close to the window, only a narrow alley in between. She would surely hurt herself dropping down into the alley. And then there would be the problem of getting out of the gate, which was likely guarded by soldiers searching for Tobie. So, Lucy turned her attention to finding a way across to the wall.

Reaching back inside, she carefully pulled a bench up, and pushed it out through the window. The wall was slightly higher than the window, but the bench spanned the opening nicely. Checking that the up-side-down bench was stable, Lucy drew a breath to strengthen her nerves for the dangerous feat ahead.

She had a good head for heights, but her heart drummed loudly in her ears as she shinned across the wooden bench, holding her white muslin skirt in her teeth to keep it out of the way. Blushing as she gained the wall, Lucy looked back at the castle to see if any faces were turned her way. The stone edifice with its apertures, crenellations and turrets glared silently back at her, and she breathed a sigh of relief that no one had witnessed her unladylike folly.

Lucy pulled the bench from its position on the ledge and let it drop with a crash to the alley below. *Now no one can follow, not until they have a ladder of some sort. By then I'll be far away.*

Sheltered on both sides by high crenellations, Lucy sped along the wall-walk, moving northwards. The sun was shrouded with heavy, dull clouds, but she could tell by its illusive brightness which direction it was just now.

Ahead, Lucy spied a place where the path below was not so far from the wall-top. *About two of me...* she calculated, and as she moved on further, she realized that the ground sloped away.

The wall took a turn ahead, and Lucy guessed that around the corner the gatehouse towers would block her way. *I must make good the opportunity, now, before they find I've left the chamber and begin looking for me. But, if Tobie discovers I'm out of the castle...*

Moving back to where the ground seemed closest, Lucy listened for any sound of horses or people. The air was sultry and she wondered if it might rain. Gathering the hem of her skirt and tucking it into her thin belt, Lucy checked that her key was still attached, and sighed in relief when she found it was. In her haste, she had almost forgotten this asset. She would most certainly need it to collect her carry-bag from the royal mausoleum.

Lucy drew a deep breath. *I must land on my feet, and bend at the knees...and it won't be hay that I tumble on.*

She jumped.

Falling forward on her knees, Lucy extended her hands to prevent herself falling on her face. She brushed the gravel from her hands, then her knees, knowing the damage was slight. *All I've done is graze my hands and knees!*

Only twice before in her life had woods appeared so inviting, and Lucy, breathing more freely, lost herself among the trees.

Moving down the slope, she listened to the singing of the birds growing quiet as she approached. Waiting for some minutes until they resumed their twittering songs, Lucy removed her leather shoes. Tying the laces together, she slung them over her shoulder and trod silently towards her chosen destination, listening as she moved.

I'll go to Lord Tullus' cottage, and if no one is living there, I'll sleep there tonight. My hidden trunk will supply a new identity if needed. Tomorrow, I must fetch my carry-bag and buy food. Maybe I'll contact Tage and the girls...

Remembering her conversation with Shalone, Lucy wondered, H*ow can there be a purpose? What reason is there that I should feel so afraid that I have to flee and hide my identity? It makes no sense at all. I just feel guilty, all over again...*

Chapter Fourteen

The trek in the woods beneath the perimeter of the city wall, was a much longer and slower exercise than Lucy had imagined. Melville Castle was more than a mile from the city gates in one direction, while Tullus Hall was in the other. In between were diverse tracks, paths and roads—and many hidden dangers, which Lucy realized, when she trod close to a band of thieves counting their takings from the previous night. Their laughter and uncontrolled frivolity came from having emptied the large number of wine flasks strewn about them.

Swiftly retracing her steps, but maintaining her stealth, Lucy was thankful, yet amazed that the celebrating thieves had not been diligent enough to post a lookout. She shivered, knowing that Tobie would likely socialize with such people.

She took the road until hoof-beats warned of approaching horses. It was a military company, and Lucy was torn between speaking to them or remaining hidden. Choosing the latter, she thought of the new king who would be in deep mourning for his father.

He won't want to be bothered with a 'Lucy' turning up now, she reasoned dolefully. *If only I had known about Father before I met the prince at my secret pool. How can it be that there's a reason in it all when I have been so foolish? Is it possible that God can take our mistakes and turn them into something meaningful? Oh, dear God,* she prayed, *If only you could...*

Shadows were lengthening when the cottage came in sight.

Fear tightened Lucy's throat as she imagined that Lord Tullus' footmen would be there, waiting for 'Widow Winnie'.

They're not likely to leave such a place unlocked or unchecked all night...and what if someone else is living there now?

Lucy reached the thicket where her trunk was hidden. Unlocking the trunk, she pulled out a gray 'widow-wig'. With experienced fingers, she rearranged her plaits around her head and pulled the wig over the top. Peering into the mirror on her make-up box, Lucy skillfully added lines and age to her face. Noting that her white dress was badly in need of a wash, Lucy pulled out a twin dress, then a gray widow's dress, a wrinkled mask, and a cloak with matching bonnet. Having donned the fresh white dress and covered it with the gray, she placed the other items in the trunk at the top and locked it. Lucy would have stepped out, but the sound of hoof-beats caused her to remain motionless.

Three men wearing the distinctive Tullus uniform dismounted, and Lucy watched while one man, after scanning the immediate area, lifted a flat stone near the steps and snatched up a key. Entering and checking the cottage briefly before replacing the key and riding off, the guards were obviously on a circuit of the estate, checking the nearby woods for poachers as they rode. Lucy wondered at this guard, which had not bothered the two nights they had slept there. Perhaps it was something new.

How often do they come? Maybe I'd better sleep here in the thicket. She sniffed the air, and again felt that moisture blew in the light breeze. *I want to sleep in a real bed...*

Gingerly retrieving the key from under the stone, and opening the front door, Lucy entered the cottage just as the sun sank to its rest for the day. Unbolting a pair of shutters at the front of the house, she pushed them outward, and swung herself over the sill. Locking the front door again, Lucy placed the key in its hiding place and climbed back in the window.

Moving to the bedchamber where Tage had slept, she sighed and tried unsuccessfully to resist the urge to sleep upon a real feather mattress.

One night will be worth it, even if I'm discovered, Lucy decided. *Surely, as Lucretia Melville, Lord Tullus would not prevent me from sleeping in this bed? But perhaps I should go to the Grand House and turn myself in. It would be good to see the children.* Then Lucy remembered Tobie, and she decided to remain hidden. *When I do give in, I'll have to reveal that I was both Winnie and Mary—so I must wait until Tobie is safely in custody. Please, God, perhaps you can find reason in it all; I can't. All I'm doing is making a muddle of everything!*

Lucy did not wake before dawn, and it was the sound of hoof-beats that roused her. They were followed by boots pounding on the wooden steps at the front. Lucy leapt nimbly out of the bed, smoothed it over, and lay down beneath the coverlet on the far side.

The footsteps grew louder and the bedroom door was flung open, then closed. Only when the sound of hoof beats returned did Lucy exhale in great relief. What a deep sleep she had indulged in! What would she do now? Where could she go? To whom could she turn? *I have no one,* Lucy thought sadly, then recalled her prayers in the chapel. *But I now have You, Lord Jesus. You are my mediator, my go-between. So please, Jesus, ask Your Father to help me. I really don't know what to do next.*

Lucy remembered she had told God she would serve Him; and she had promised to tell the truth! But here she was, wearing widow's weeds, living the same lie.

Unable to prevent herself, Lucy burst into tears. She felt a deep urge to give herself up to the Lord, but fear rose within her and she felt defeated. *I want to trust You, God. I* do *trust You, but I'm afraid. Oh God, this fear is greater than my trust, and it is winning. Please, God, in spite of my fear, please help me find a way out of my doubts...*

***

The bent old widow woman, dressed in gray, hobbling dejectedly along the street to the marketplace, drew a few stray glances, but no eye lingered, for Lucy, wearing the ugly wrinkled mask, looked much older than the description of the missing Lady Winifred Melville. No resemblance to either Lucy or Mary, both being sought, could be seen in the gait of the old crone. Lucy, pausing at the notice board, was neither amused nor surprised to see she was posted there as three separate people. The thought that she could rightfully apply for the rewards offered for all three, brought no feeling of mirth.

Glancing around the area, fully expecting someone waiting to capture her, Lucy's attention moved back to the newly mounted notice about the criminal Tobie, previous night watchman at Melville Castle. He was wanted alive for interrogation, and described as very dangerous. Lucy was angry, wishing he was listed as wanted 'Dead or Alive'.

She shuddered. *How can I be safe while he's on the prowl? Unless I remain hidden, he'll find me—he seemed such a ferret...*

Finding a suitable shaped branch to use as a walking stick, Lucy, her head turned to the ground, tapped her way along the main street, intending to go to the mausoleum to collect her carry-bag. Though she was both hungry and thirsty, she knew she must not hurry. She must act the part of a frail, aged woman.

The palace gates were open and a slow-moving queue grew longer by the minute. Lucy hovered long enough to hear that the people were permitted to pay respects to the late king. He was lying-in-state in the great throne room.

I'll come back later, Lucy promised herself as she shuffled slowly away. *I must get money to buy food. I'll feel better when I've eaten... and I'll be safe from Tobie in the palace...perhaps I'll see the prince...* Then she thought bitterly, *For what reason would I see him? What purpose could there be in that?*

A guard of a dozen men surrounded the royal mausoleum, and Lucy faltered on past, knowing it was impossible to enter just now. Moving close to the wall, she wondered if she might find some drinking water. She remembered the well in the square, surrounded by thirsty commoners impatient for their turn. Lucy disliked drinking at the public well—even being near such a place—where frequent quarrels and brawls broke out as those too poor to buy cider or wine line up for a free drink.

Finding nowhere to relieve her thirst, and the way becoming narrow and dingy, Lucy retraced her steps to the royal mausoleum. A long cart was drawn up outside and soldiers were carefully lifting a beautifully crafted marble slab. Although other men were added to carry the heavy object, the going was slow and tedious.

Joining the small crowd, Lucy watched for a few minutes before someone's comment made her realize she would not be able to collect her coins for some time.

"They're preparing the place alongside the queen. They've got to bring several side pieces just like that, also the lid, then the effigy," one woman told another.

"I heard that the elf...effery...thing...was made two years ago when the king was first sick."

Too thirsty to linger, Lucy quickened her pace to reach the well before she fainted in the heat. The sky was cloudy, the air oppressive, and Lucy remembered she wore two dresses under the heavy cloak. She longed to remove the outer garment, but a widow-woman was not properly dressed without her cloak and bonnet. The blue eyes beneath the false wrinkles eyed maidens in their loose muslin dresses with envy.

The noon hour passed before Lucy quenched her thirst, and she turned her attention to visiting the palace before returning to her trunk at the cottage. She fervently hoped to discover a penny or two somewhere amongst her varied belongings in the trunk. How unfortunate that she had taken all her savings in the carry-bag, but the trunk had not seemed a safe place for the fifteen silver ducat and many pennies. Five ducats could purchase an average horse, and a cart could be added for two more! Lucy's hopes for survival were in that carry bag, pushed behind a royal baby's statue in the royal mausoleum.

What do you want me to do, God? Lucy asked, *Shall I go to the Grand House, or shall I go to the palace?* She felt hungry and weary, so the Grand House seemed a welcome place to be. *I should have gone there last evening. Something now is drawing me to the palace—I'll feel less fearful in the palace,* she told herself, and grimaced, thinking, *I want to go there because I'll feel safe there. Tobie would never go into the palace...*

***

Garlicky aromas wafted from Lucy's garments and people in the line kept a distance from the wizened old woman, which pleased Lucy. The mask, which fitted closely over her nose and around her mouth, was made of fabric coated with wet clay, and had a drooping, hooked nose, many wrinkles, and several large warts on the dropped chin. Make-up had been applied and gray hairs were stuck on the eyebrows and chin. Fuzzy, silvery hair from the wig protruded from the bonnet, covering Lucy's eyes and providing a misty veil for her brilliant blue orbs peering furtively in all directions.

An hour advanced monotonously. Quiet, interesting conversations buzzed around her, and Lucy drew closer and closer to the chamber were she would view the King's body. *It's the least I can do. King Lothar thought so much of Father...he'll rest close by...and I do feel so safe here, even with guards all around...* but again the thought intruded, *the prince is somewhere in this vast place.*

Eavesdropping without shame, Lucy listened to three middle-aged women in front, discussing the now deceased king, the late queen, and the new king, Lothar. Seeking to outdo one another with their 'factual' royal knowledge, they spoke of the times they had seen the young prince, and how very grieved he had been over his mother's death. Lucy smiled secretively as they spoke of the "golden-haired maiden" for whom the prince had been searching. When a younger woman in line ahead of the three, however, turned and joined the conversation, Lucy's amusement turned sour.

"I heard that they *knowed* who she is!" The woman became center of attention. "Yes." She leaned back on the wall of the palace entrance hall where the queue was directed. A black silken cord, a few feet from the wall, confined the line, allowing palace officials, guards and staff to come and go without hindrance.

"Lady Lucretia Melville!" the woman announced triumphantly, making Lucy tremble. "The daughter of that lord who's layin' in the royal mausoleum. She be about eighteen or nineteen years, and very beaut'ful." The three women grouped around the younger, listening eagerly, as was another young lady hidden under widows-weeds. "I speak the truth, I do." The woman turned and looked at the line ahead, stepping backwards to fill the gap, and hushed her tone. Lucy closed the gap between them and, as she eavesdropped, her heart beat faster.

"My neighbor has a sister wot works for that Lord Tullus. Well, it seems that Lord Melville's wife be alive, too, as well as his daughter. Mind, it isn't known abroad yet, so don't speak of it." The women drew closer to the gossip, all exclaiming in undertones, and asking questions. Some of their answers were lost in the prattle.

The women all drew back, astounded, as a statement was made. "Blind?" "Deaf?" Lucy heard the questioning exclamations. Then, "Poor little children! All injured in that dreaded raid. And you say the young lord is so crippled he can't walk straight?"

The center of the women's attention spoke excitedly now, and others joined the group. Lucy found herself shunted closer.

"Evidently a doctor said, given time, he can fix the young lad's leg, but not so for the blind girl; and the oldest was rendered quite speechless or some'it near to it. Both bright, pretty things, I'm told..."

Compassion-filled tones flowed from the following sentences; then Lucy learned that the littlest girl, Jane-Belle Melville, had given Lord Tullus the clue that Lucretia Melville was still alive.

"Evidently, the little one—they call her Jaybee, imagine! Well, she said that the maid, Lucy, was with Widow Winifred. Mind, they don't give their aunt a respectful title, all the children call her 'Winnie'. Anyway, the little girl said that the last time she saw Lucy, who is Lucretia her cousin, was back in Passcau at a shack they lived in. Lord Tullus has sent a company to find her and bring her to Tullus Hall."

Lucy smiled and continued the slow movement, straining her ears, listening, as they now moved along a beautiful corridor. Dear little Jaybee. She had spoken the truth. The last time the little girl had seen Lucy—as Lucy—was at Donal's shack in Passcau.

Suddenly, the line moved faster and they found themselves ascending a wide stairway. Again, a thick cord confined their passage.

Here, an angry palace attendant confronted the women, reprimanding them, "This is a time of solemn commiseration. How dare you use this grievous moment for gossip. If you do not silence yourselves, you will be escorted out!"

The women dispersed and were silent until they were well out of sight of this man, and then the three ahead of Lucy spoke only in muffled undertones.

***

The throne room was sectioned into space for commoners to pass fairly close to the King's casket, but the area around the bier was roped-off for the nobility.

The foyer to the throne room was also divided, forcing the women to walk single file. A wide passage had been allowed on the other side, obviously for those of the nobility who would be leaving, having entered by a side door. A herald announced the nobility as they entered the throne room.

Lucy started as she saw Cynthia walk past, holding Jaybee's hand. She would not have recognized Jaybee in her lovely dress, if Cynthia had not been with her. Next came Avalyn, resplendent in a beautiful outfit, her hair arranged as Lucy had never seen it, walking close to the rope, moving near to where Lucy stood.

The blind girl held Yolanda's hand tightly, but Lucy saw her blind cousin pause and turn her way. *She can smell my garlic!* Lucy realized, with a sense of panic. *This is not the place for a reunion.*

Lucy did not wish to be seen by Yolanda who would surely recognize the mask, so she turned and moved closer to the larger woman in front. However, a few minutes later, when Tage stepped into the foyer, some paces ahead of Lord and Lady Tullus, Lucy hissed at him.

"Tage..."

The lad turned and stared at the owner of the voice. His eyes lit up with recognition and he stepped toward her. Lucy shook her head and he turned as though he had not seen her.

He did, however, back close to the cord and stare into the throne room as though taking a last glimpse of the late king.

Unbending a little and raising her chin so she spoke into his ear, Lucy whispered, "The cottage...where we first slept...come, after dark...we'll talk...and...and...I need to pray with you. I...I...the Lord God...He found me at last..." She would have added more, but Lord and Lady Tullus had halted their exit, obviously waiting for Tage to move on. But Tage was strangely still with a light in his eyes and a glad smile spreading across his handsome young face.

Jostled from behind, Lucy found herself moving into the incredible Lotharingian Throne Room. She drew a trembling breath at the sight of numerous military uniforms. Shoulder-to-shoulder, around the great chamber, stood soldiers in their scarlet jackets. Instead of white trousers, they wore black. Each wore a black crisscross sash on his chest, and a matching band about his right arm. Their scarlet hats and plumes had been replaced with black, and were held under their left arms.

King Lothar lay in an open casket placed on a bier. Lucy, as she gazed upon his bearded profile, thought of him as being asleep. Several women crossed themselves and moved away. Lucy shuffled to an area where people were kneeling and praying. No one was hurried through this great chamber and, in spite of the many guards, Lucy experienced a feeling of peace and serenity.

How long she stood, both contemplating and gazing, she had no idea. Her mind was focused upon the conversation she had overheard, remembering the closeness of a father and son. Now that son had lost his father; a father; a king; a man who had been a close friend to her own father. And she could not speak to him, for like her father, he was dead. She longed to talk to the king about her father. Then, she wondered how Prince Lothar was faring in his sorrow. Once she had been in the same position as the prince, having lost her father, but her situation had seemed one of shame and degradation, not of honor and glory. Prince Lothar was no longer prince, but king, the last of a dynasty unless he married and produced an heir...

An air-current blew into the throne room and Lucy shivered, despite being too warm. Movement near the entrance doors attracted her attention, and she heard a guard commanding an old man to remove his hat. Something about the “old man” drew a second look from Lucy. She was not immediately sure what it was until, after having gingerly removed his hat, he patted and stroked the hair on his head before strolling into the chamber and stepping closer to the black cord surrounding the bier and dividing the common people from the nobility.

The truth was like icy water thrown in Lucy’s face and she recoiled. Her hand flew to cover her mouth for fear she would cry out.

That man...I’m sure he wears a wig...and...he has the build of a much younger man. He walks...his clothes...

Lucy’s nerves prickled as she remembered someone else, exactly like that, save the wig, an evil young man who had walked ahead of her, and turned to confront her with a dagger...

Chapter Fifteen

"His Majesty, King Lothar, the Fourth, of Lotharingia!"

Lucy jumped as the deep voice filled the great throne room.

She froze, mindless for a moment then realized that those around her were moving. Men bowed, women curtsied low. Lucy nervously bobbed a curtsy, emulating an old woman in her jerky action. Extremely nervous, she almost dropped to her knees.

Lothar, wearing the black costume of a prince in mourning, entered the throne room, followed by members of the court.

Lucy recognized Ludwig, who moved to stand on the far side of the bier. He was almost facing her, and his eyes moved deliberately about the chamber, searching for someone. He frowned at her, then set his glassy stare in a slightly different direction. Lucy grimaced, perturbed by the macabre fixation of Ludwig's face.

Ludwig seems to have taken the King's death extremely hard, Lucy thought, and she wondered how Prince Lothar was faring.

The heir to the throne stood close to the bier, his back to Lucy; and she saw he struggled to control his emotions. His shoulders heaved a little, and then squared before he bowed his head.

Focusing her eyes beyond the King's son, Lucy again caught the weird concentrated stare on Ludwig's face. His eyelids flickered closed briefly and he crossed himself. Lucy shuddered involuntarily, for he made the motion backwards. His right hand dropped from his forehead, clenched in a fist over his heart as though he felt a dreadful pain; while at the same time, he gave just the trace of a nod.

Lucy's heart jumped at the undeniable impression that this was a preplanned signal. Her eyes flew to the man who stood by the cord directly behind Prince Lothar. Her gaze moved from the matted gray wig to his clean-shaven profile, knowing it was the face of the criminal, Tobie. His fingers crept unpretentiously beneath his cloak, and Lucy saw him slide a dagger from the folds. He held the long, silver blade erect, a manner she recognized. With a deft movement, Tobie lifted the dagger to shoulder-height, then twisted, taking aim...

"*No*! *No*!" Lucy shouted, her hand out as though to prevent the flight of the missile. Realizing her inability to save the motionless prince, she projected a shrill scream, shattering the tranquility of the solemn moment.

As the dagger flew, Prince Lothar turned, frowning deeply at the ear-splitting scream. The knife, instead of lodging deeply in the center of the prince's back, sank into the muscle of his left arm, piercing the bone. The prince gasped loudly and sank to his knees, his right hand on the dagger handle. Lucy saw the bright color of blood oozing through his fingers.

Pandemonium broke out as shrieks and shouts intermingled with the unsheathing of swords and pounding boots and shoes on the marble. Panicking people cowered away in all directions.

Frozen to the spot, Lucy realized the dagger had been aimed at the prince's heart and, given the length of the blade, would have penetrated that organ through his back if he had not turned.

A soldier with sword drawn rushed Tobie, who was trying to become anonymous, slinking into the crowd. Lucy gasped as the criminal turned toward her. Although knowing he did not recognize her, she felt vulnerable. Without hesitation, the guard slashed at the murderer, the sword slicing deep into his left shoulder and down his arm. Tobie dropped to his knees, crying out for mercy. The guard kicked him in the face, causing him to fall backwards unconscious. Blood poured from the massive gash, forming a pool on the marble. Lucy's eyes darted across to the crowd of attendants and guards rushing to the prince's aid. Surrounded by palace guards, several attendants lifted the injured prince carefully, preparing to carry him out. Shouts for the throne room to be cleared repeated and soldiers herded men and women out the side door.

As Lucy's gaze followed the prince's departure, a man stepped into the path of her view. Ludwig! Through the silver mist of her wig hair, she saw agitation on Ludwig's face. He stared directly at her as if afraid that she had seen his signal.

Bowing her head, Lucy hastened to close the space between her and the departing commoners.

"That woman! Seize her! The old woman!" Ludwig shouted, pointing, stepping in her direction.

Lucy had lingered long enough to be separated easily from the throng by the soldiers who rushed to obey the nobleman's command. Although there was no escape, Lucy backed away from the two guards who reached for her. Her struggle was brief, and she could not find her tongue to scream again.

Dragged towards Ludwig, Lucy heard a deep voice protesting, "That's the woman who saved the prince's life. It was she who screamed!"

Ludwig, his sword drawn, concocted a lie, "She's the murderer's wife, his accomplice. She must die!"

Deep anger flooded Lucy, her face growing hotter under the mask. "Wife?" she questioned in a shrill tone, her anger superseding her fear. "That man is Tobie the murderer. And I'm not wife to anyone!"

"Huh? She claims the old man is Tobie?" Ludwig stepped towards Lucy, cynicism twisting his face. "If he's Tobie, then I suppose *she's* the Virgin Mary."

Ludwig, his sword raised, halted as a captain stood in his way. The uniformed man stared from Lucy to the face of the unconscious Tobie. Lucy hoped he saw that, though Tobie's hair looked old, his face was young.

"He wears a wig and...and he's shaved his beard," Lucy declared, recognizing the shrill tone of her voice. The name "Mary" vibrated in her brain and her anger increased at Ludwig's sardonic accusation. Straightening, she pointed at Ludwig and said calmly, "It's *you*, Ludwig, who are Tobie's accessory. I saw you signal him!" She looked at the captain, who for some reason was supporting her. He stared at her in a curious manner; and she realized her voice no longer matched her disguise.

“Why would Ludwig want the prince dead?” she asked no one in particular, reverting to the shrill tone. She realized by the ominous silence that followed, her words had alerted two factions in the throne room. Many here supported Ludwig, a traitor against the throne, but Lucy hoped the prince’s supporters were the greater majority.

After clearing the throne room, the guards re-deployed around the chamber, standing alert, awaiting further instructions. Their captains congregated around the unconscious assassin’s pool of blood. Lucy stared around at the many uniforms blocking any hope of escape; and a foreboding of imminent battle caused her heart to pound.

Suddenly, a captain snatched the wig from Tobie’s head. Just as quickly, another captain ran him through, and sparks flew as many swords clashed. The men along the walls joined the battle, and chaos took the Lotharingian Throne Room.

Lucy saw Ludwig advancing towards her, and deftly dodged the careless stab of his sword. He seemed surprised to see an old widow move so fast. His next slash was more controlled, and great was his astonishment when the old crone sidestepped again.

Ducking away from him, Lucy retrieved her staff from the floor, and struck at Ludwig’s shins, dodging his sword. She rolled to the marble, away from his sword arm, rolling over and over towards the bier.

Ludwig turned to engage swords with a captain, and Lucy wondered how they all knew whose side each was on? Voices shouted, calling for order, but no one obeyed the commands. Springing to her feet, Lucy moved out the only unguarded exit, following those who had carried the prince.

Above the commotion, she heard Ludwig shouting in alarm, “Stop that woman! Cut her down! She must not leave!”

Marble passages converged confusingly before Lucy as she fled. Far from the gait of an old woman, her flight was much more animated, because she knew she ran for her life!

Ludwig must have been one that the prince's father referred to! He'll not hesitate to kill me.

Lucy fled along a narrow corridor, relieved to hear the sound of battle becoming distant. *I've not gone the way they expected,* she mused, *because I have no idea where I'm going.*

There was a descending stairway ahead with palace guards coming up. They shouted for her to halt, but she chose an empty corridor instead, running towards a far-off open door. Before she reached it, however, soldiers appeared in front of her, blocking the passage.

"It's the old woman who screamed!" a soldier called. "She's a witness against Ludwig." He beckoned her, "Quick, this way!"

Thankful that her escort knew the way to take, Lucy wondered where they were going. She lost all sense of direction as they went along a corridor and up a narrow spiral stairway. On the next level, they were confronted, and swords again engaged in fierce combat.

"That door..." the young soldier pointed down a wide hallway from which guards were rushing to assist in the battle, "Hurry, tell them to lock it behind you!" He protected her retreat, stabbing and dispatching several of his attackers.

Lucy slithered one hand along the wall, keeping behind the young soldier. Her fear vanished when she saw a man, sword raised, approaching her protector from behind. Using the wooden staff, she swung at his sword hand, then clobbered the back of his neck, causing him to turn on her. Before he could strike her with his sword, he was run through. The young soldier grasped her arm and pulled her towards the doors. Two guards followed them into the room, locking the door behind them.

A large room stretched before Lucy's eyes, but before she could take in the opulent furnishings, or imagine exactly where she was, the door was hammered upon.

"Name yourself," the young soldier called.

"Chief Brigadier Marten. I demand entrance!"

"Don't let him in," the young soldier urged, "we must protect the prince."

"But he's the Chief Commander..." the second guard said, obviously confused. "Surely *he'll* protect the heir to the throne!"

Lucy backed away from the men and moved across the carpeted room. It was a massive sitting room, and around the corner there was an area with a desk by a window that took up almost the whole wall. Two more guards entered from a wide archway, and Lucy pointed to the door, saying meekly, "They're having a battle...at the door."

The men hurried toward the commotion.

Drawing aside the curtains on the other side of the arch, Lucy found a large bedchamber. The immense four-poster bed was dwarfed by the size of the room. The bed was not occupied, but three men were grouped next to a capacious couch where two of them held a man down. There was a loud moan followed a gasp of pain from the couch, and Lucy heard the clatter of a dagger on a tray. One of the men moved and she saw the prince's face.

"Prince Lothar..." Lucy whispered under her breath.

"Who are you? How did you get in here?" An attendant grasped her wrist, snatching the wooden staff from her grip.

Lucy tried to reach up under her bonnet to undo the ties of her mask, but it was impossible with one hand. "Let me go, please." she begged. She was not released, but her captor turned to hear a shout in the sitting room: "Chief Brigadier Marten requests entrance!"

It was not a request, but a demand. The Chief Brigadier stormed into the prince's bedchamber waving his bloodstained sword, causing everyone to move back and bow respectfully.

Lucy cowered away from the large-framed commander, thankful that the attendant let her go in order to bow. The wall at her back stopped her retreat, and she froze, feeling extremely vulnerable.

She breathed easier when the brigadier wiped his sword on the velvet curtain and pushed it into its sheath, his attention fixed on the prince.

Two soldiers carrying Tobie came in and dumped him at the Brigadier's feet. Four more soldiers entered with drawn swords and formed a line across the only exit; awaiting their next orders.

"Sir Ludwig," a voice announced. The soldiers parted to allow him entrance.

"Where is she?" Ludwig demanded, his eyes scanning the room before resting contemptuously on Lucy. He spat, and with his hand on the hilt of his sword, stepped toward her. "You...you...you ruined everything!"

He turned to the Chief Brigadier, "Fine idea of yours! We won't be implicated you said!" He drew his sword, looking again at Lucy, who knew from his face that she was already dead.

But, a hand on Ludwig's shoulder stopped him and he listened to the attendant's whispered message.

Lucy's heart pounded as she turned her thoughts to the prince. *Who am I, but a simple maiden? He is the heir to the throne; the hope of the kingdom. Ludwig must not kill him! Oh God, Heavenly Father, Please help the prince. Don't let Ludwig kill him!*

She thought of her own defenselessness. *Please, dear God; I don't want to die. I'm not ready to die.* Though her eyes were wide open with fear, Lucy prayed within her soul, *Give me courage, Lord, and if I can help Lothar, then show me how.* An overwhelming feeling that she should have been at his side, long before now, swamped her. *He wanted me...and I could have helped him. I should have come forward, when we came to Verdun...*

Now, it all seemed so impossible.

With trembling hands, Lucy loosened the mask and bonnet, but did not remove them. She was sure the time would come, but how could her revelation save the prince? It might, at best, be a distraction for a short time only. Her breath came tumultuously with the dread thought that nothing could save him. That is, nothing but God's intervention. *I must pray...*

The attendant's voice was pleading, "The King's counselors are coming, Sir, they wish to speak with you, to negotiate. You must not do anything rash at this stage, Sir."

The Chief Brigadier spoke, "Lothar's not going anywhere. Let's take counsel, Ludwig." He pointed his sword at Tobie. "I still believe Tobie can be given full blame, that's why I had him brought here. But just to be sure..." He strode close to the unconscious form and plunged his sword deep into the man's chest. The body jerked as Marten withdrew his weapon, and then was still.

Turning, Marten looked at the prince, saying, "We hold the trophy while we hold this room secure." He directed his sword at the attendants standing close to the couch. "If you don't move out, I'll have my men take you out feet first!"

Not one man moved. Though unarmed, they were prepared to die protecting their prince. One younger man snatched the dagger from the tray, but before he could turn, the Chief Brigadier plunged his sword into his back. "Take them out!" he commanded.

Prince Lothar, his arm in a sling, struggled to sit. "Don't harm my loyal friends..."

Clenching his fist, the Chief Brigadier punched the prince on the jaw, forcing him backward on the couch. He was still, and Lucy felt strangely thankful, sure the large commander would have punched him again if he had moved. The attendants were carried from the room.

Lucy cringed as the Chief Brigadier turned to her. She saw the glint in Ludwig's eye, his raised sword, his gesture, and found herself grasped by two burly soldiers and thrown bodily to sprawl at his feet. Fully expecting to feel pain before death, Lucy felt the floor spinning beneath her as she tried to gather her wits.

"What's this?" Ludwig snatched up the mask, then the bonnet as it fell off. Lucy looked up at him. He stared at the mask in disbelief. "*The widow!*"

Lucy knew it had dawned upon the traitor that she was the same woman he had confronted, over two weeks ago, near Passcau. She was dragged to her feet, the soldiers all speaking at once.

Hammering sounded from the adjoining room and a guard yelled, "They're trying to break down the door! They want proof that the prince is still alive."

Releasing Lucy with a shove, Ludwig sprang toward the arches, saying, "Come, we'll bargain. Guard this room. The prince must be confined here! And guard this woman!"

"Yes," the Commander interjected, "she'll be useful. The coconspirator to the crime of the murder of the King Elect..."

Chapter Sixteen

Lucy felt alienated from the real world.

An idea wriggled around in her mind, like a moth wanting to break out of its cocoon, and she knew anything was worth a try. But could she carry out such a plan? And how could she distract the guards? How much time did she have before Ludwig returned? The hammering had ceased. Surely, the buzz of voices in the next room could not mean the bargaining of life or death for the king of Lotharingia! How could they consider anything other than supporting the heir to the throne?

Lucy knew Tobie was dead. A large red patch soaked the carpet around the murderer, and his face had a strange blue-white appearance. The two guards just stared at her. Spying a pitcher of water, Lucy poured herself a drink and swallowed it in a few gulps, not fully aware that she had quenched her thirst.

"Perhaps the prince needs a drink," a guard at her shoulder urged. Recoiling, Lucy met his eyes before turning to stare at the other guard. *They support the prince!* she thought. *Please, dear God, help them to rescue him...he must not be murdered, please, God.*

As though reading her mind, the guard said, "We're outnumbered, but if there is something we can do to get him away to safety... If we can get to the king's chamber, there's a secret passage..."

"It goes to the mausoleum?" Lucy asked.

"How did you know that?"

Lucy did not answer. She looked down at Tobie again. Kneeling down, she listened to his chest. No sound came to her ears.

"I've an idea," Lucy whispered, "If you do as I say, we may save the prince's life. Quickly! Switch the two. Change the prince's clothes with Tobie's. Hurry! I'll work on their faces..."

The soldiers stared at her as though she had gone mad. "Perhaps you have a better idea?" She gave them a brief moment, and then explained, "If we exchange the two, they'll think the prince is dead, but it'll be Tobie. You can drag the prince out as if you're taking the traitor to a dungeon or somewhere. That way, our prince...our *king*...can escape."

Snatching the razor-sharp dagger from the floor, Lucy prayed for steadiness of hand as she deftly shaved the prince's moustache, and then cut a small handful of his hair. She was glad he did not wake, and pleased to see his chest rising and falling evenly.

The guards had not done as she asked, but stood on either side, watching her gravely as if wondering about her intentions.

"I am Lucretia Melville," she said. "The late Lord Terrance Melville's daughter. If you would save our king, you must change his clothes with Tobie's. I'll make a moustache with the prince's hair and put it on Tobie." Seeing their continued doubt, she added, "People see what they expect to see. I'm proof of that!

"When Ludwig returns, he'll believe they're both dead. The attention will be on the prince, who will be Tobie. Until a doctor, or someone who knows him well—like Ludwig—sees him, a few minutes could mean his life. You'll have to get the prince out as quickly as possible, without arousing suspicion." She watched as the men obeyed her, pulling off Tobie's sandals and unlacing his bloodstained tunic.

There was a loud argument in the sitting room and Lucy heard Ludwig's voice over top of the Chief Brigadier's. She prayed they would not burst in here.

When Tobie was dressed in the prince's clothes and lay dead on the couch, Lucy fixed the sling on his arm. Taking a lighted candle, she drizzled hot wax on his upper lip before using the prince's hair to form a moustache. She trimmed Tobie's unruly hair with the dagger, gathering the cut locks on a hand towel before combing his hair with her fingers. She used water from the pitcher to both arrange the hair on Tobie's forehead in a similar manner to the prince's, and to make it appear darker.

One of the guards whispered urgently, "Your Highness, you must lie still. Ludwig and Marten have betrayed you. Ludwig wants your throne. No, Sire, you must lie down! Please don't think you can confront them..."

The other guard knelt down to help restrain Lothar. "Please, Sire, you *must* pretend to be unconscious. There's murder in the minds of Sir Ludwig and Brigadier Marten, and they have men who obey them, Sire..."

The prince asked, "Whose clothes am I wearing?" He lifted his hand to the bruise on his jaw, then to his naked upper lip, asking, "What are you doing to me?"

Lucy knelt as she spoke, "We wish to help you escape death, Sire. We've changed you for someone else so we can help you..."

"Ludwig wants to kill me?" he asked. "He's my friend...I confided in him...how wrong I was about him...all is lost...Father was right to fear..." His eyes focused on Lucy's face. "Who are you?"

In the light of the torches, Lucy could see the green in his hazel eyes. She reprimanded herself for thinking of his eyes at a time like this. "I am Lucretia Melville, Your Highness. I introduced myself as Lucy to you in the forest. Do you remember? I was the widow, Sire. I'm wearing a wig."

She blushed, reaching up under the gray hair and pulling out hairpins while still speaking in her soft voice, "All is not lost, Sire. We're here to help you. With God's help, you will escape." She looked across to one of the soldiers. "There must be many more faithful Lotharingian men out there who will lend our king their help."

The astonished prince watched Lucy pull the wig from her head. "Lucy?" He said, reaching out to touch her cheek lightly, a gentle caress, as if to confirm she were real. "Lucy? Can it really be you?"

"Yes, Your Highness. I'm Lucy. Lucretia was the name that you did not think of when...when we met in the forest..." Her eyes met his and she was silent, transfixed for a moment, and then she said, "I can't take time to explain it all now, Your Highness, but my idea is to exchange you with Tobie who is dead. They'll carry *you* away thinking you are *him*."

She saw his eyebrows knit into a frown, and exclaimed, "His eyebrows! They're much too thick! Lie down, in case they come." She stood, swallowing, speaking to herself, "I have to touch him...Tobie...again..."

The prince saw her shudder as she moved away. This time, when the two guards pushed him backwards on the floor, he obeyed, but propped himself up on his right arm, watching Lucy.

"She screamed. Yes, I remember that scream...and she was the widow at Passcau." He then spoke to the soldier kneeling on one knee before him, "Is this the only way? Can we not resist?"

"No, Sire. Not unless there are more of us. It's difficult because we obey the Commander, believing he works for your good. And you're weak from blood loss and not sleeping while sitting with your father. We think your sitting room is filled with traitors, Sire. There may be one or two who'd support you, but most out there are Sir Ludwig's men, and the Brigadier's cohorts obey their leader without question."

"Let's do it this way for now, Sire," the other soldier urged. "It'll give us time, if we can get you out of your chambers and can keep Ludwig's mind off you here. Tobie may fool them in your clothes as long as they don't look at you closely, so you must not move, Sire, not a twinge!"

The room next door had grown quiet. The time it took to set the scene seemed an age to Lucy. She moved around the room, blowing out the two nearest candles to make the room dimmer. The afternoon was dull and little light filtered in through the high bedroom windows.

What would I do if this truly was Prince—King—Lothar? she asked herself. Holding her wig in one hand, Lucy knelt before the couch. Reaching out, she touched the hand of the murderer. Trembling, she bowed her head and prayed.

The room was swiftly invaded and the guard closest to Lothar kicked the prince's elbow, removing his 'prop'. Lucy turned slowly, looking up to meet Ludwig's eyes. The Chief Brigadier, his sword drawn, stood by Ludwig's side.

"He's dead," she said simply, not knowing that her face and wig-less hair had saved her life at that moment. The two men just stared: Ludwig at Lucy, Marten at Tobie; their faces as vacant as executioners. Then, recognition dawned in their eyes.

Ludwig spoke, "*You!* How on earth did you get in here?" He turned to Marten, "It's that maiden Lucy." His saw the wig in her hand and said lamely, "You are...you were...the widow..."

The Chief Brigadier was still staring at the form on the couch. "Lothar is dead?" This revelation seemed to hit him in much the same way as the discovery of stolen treasure would. Sheathing his sword, he shoved Lucy out of the way, knelt, and listened to Tobie's chest. As he felt around Tobie's neck, seeking the jugular vein, he said, "Call a doctor. I-I think Lothar is dead!" He lifted trembling, clumsy fingers to Tobie's nostrils. "He's not breathing and there's no pulse. He is dead. He's still warm, though."

"Did you kill him?" Ludwig asked Lucy.

"I did not," Lucy replied, standing. She knew the prince's close companion would know it wasn't the prince on the couch, so to keep Ludwig's attention from Tobie, she raised her chin, held her head high, and stared directly at Ludwig. "My name is Lucretia Melville."

"Light the room!" Ludwig commanded, stepping close to Lucy.
Marten's deep voice trembled as if he still did not believe the reality of the body before him. "No. Leave it dim. It's more appropriate. The doctors must be fetched. And not that simpleton Weber! Fetch Astor. Then summon the King's counselors and the Court."

He stood to face Ludwig. "The deed is done for us, Ludwig. The Kingdom is ours! And it's just as I wanted: his blood is not on *our* hands." He looked contemptuously at Lucy. "The people *will* have someone to blame, so we have no more worries. Lothar is dead, and you shall be king, Ludwig!"

"Yes!" Ludwig spoke triumphantly. "At last! How often I wished him dead, and now I'm free of him! Gone are his philosophical ways and his morbid, confusing religion. And his prayers and his worship of a God who can't even be seen. How I've longed to end his tiresome quotations, his frivolous verses, his talk of eternity. Well, he's there now! If we'd not seen Lucy in the woods, the deed would have been done then. Soon we shall rid this kingdom of all religious parasites!"

Dropping on one knee before Lucy, Ludwig cried, "I am to be king of Lotharingia!" He snatched Lucy's hands, kissing them, holding them tightly as she tried to free herself; "You shall be my queen, Lucy."

"*Never!*" Lucy cried, sidestepping and twisting her body to escape his grasp. Ludwig stared open-mouthed up at her, not comprehending her refusal.

Like a dart to her heart, Lucy's eyes met Lothar's. He was trying to sit up from his position on the floor, but the guard pressed him down with his boot on his chest. Lucy realized the malignant threat to his life. *They'll kill us if they find out we've tricked them.*

Her eyes met those of another guard and she knew by his open-mouthed stare first at her, then at the prince, he understood the charade.

"Please, this room is a chamber of death. Can we not speak of it some other place, some other time?" Lucy asked, no longer struggling against Ludwig's grip, but moving closer to him.

The Chief Brigadier now took command, saying, "Yes. That's wise, Ludwig, we've enough to deal with." His eyes searched Lucy's young face. "You'll be perfect, my dear. The people will need a public example." Speaking to the guard, he commanded, "Fetch Captain Bolls." His eyes dropped to the prince. "Take the traitor's body to a dungeon for now. Perhaps we'll hang him, too! Don't announce that Tobie is dead. A public hanging for two..."

"What are you saying?" Ludwig confronted Marten. "Lucy's mine! I want her with me tonight!"

Lucy saw Prince Lothar struggle as the men, one each side, began to drag him out. Shaking her head at Lothar, she said, "I'm not yours, Ludwig. I'd rather die than be your...your..." She could not say ‘queen’ as she watched the third guard, who moved to help with the ‘body’.

“What are you saying?” Ludwig repeated. “How dare you!”

Marten strode to the curtains, crossing behind the guards bearing the prince who had now ceased his resistance. “Bolls! Bring two!”

Ludwig turned to the dead body, but it was not the face that held his attention, it was the limp right hand. “The seal ring! I must have the ring!”

Remembering Tobie’s hardened hands and filthy fingernails, Lucy spoke loudly, “You cannot have the seal ring. It’s not on his finger.” She recalled seeing at least three rings on the prince’s hands. She added, “*None* of the rings are on his fingers.” She drew in a deep breath as Ludwig bent over the murderer, pushing the sling away from the wrist, feeling the fingers, then searching each finger of the right hand. He appeared greatly disturbed that the lifeless fingers were ringless. *People see what they assume. Please, God, don’t let Ludwig see Tobie. Please blind his mind that the body is someone other than the prince.*

“This woman, take her to the interrogation cell and guard her well,” Marten commanded the men who entered the room.

Ludwig hurried to Lucy’s side, snatched her hands, and examined them. Gripping her shoulders, he shook her the way someone would shake green fruit off a tree. “What have you done with the rings?” he demanded.

Lucy struggled to free herself, but his grip tightened. “I don’t have them,” she cried.

Marten became concerned about the rings also. “The guards! The ones who took the traitor’s body...”

But Ludwig’s attention was still on Lucy. Reaching to the neck of her cloak, he wrenched it with all his might. The old, gray fabric tore and he flung the cloak to the floor. He then grasped the material of her dress. The garment tore as Lucy pulled away, leaving the front section of the gray dress in Ludwig’s hands.

“Where have you put the rings?” Ludwig was a man obsessed. “*My* rings!” The white muslin dress was revealed beneath the gray. “Take her downstairs and guard her well! I shall follow soon to make sure she does not have the rings on her. Fetch the guards...the ones who had the murderer...”

“They didn’t take the rings,” Lucy said.

“You know where they are, don’t you?” Ludwig’s eyes had fire in them. “The seal ring, the ring to the kingdom, you know where it is, don’t you, Miss Melville?”

“Yes. I know where it is,” Lucy lifted her chin defiantly, knowing discussion about the ring would give the prince more time. “It...” She glanced around the room, away from the couch, saying, “It is where the prince put it...”

“He hid it?” Ludwig asked. “Where did he hide it? Did *you* hide it for him, before he died? Where did *you* hide it?”

The room was quiet as a tomb. Possession of the seal ring was the means by which one could prove rights to the kingship of Lotharingia. King Lothar had given it into his son’s care just before he died. Ludwig needed the ring to authenticate his succession to the throne. He planned to tell the chief counselors that the prince gave it to him, along with the rights to the throne.

Lucy sighed. The prince should be somewhere safe by now. *I hope he is well enough to rally his men to gain the palace back from these traitors.* Her eyes continued to rove the room and Ludwig began searching a sideboard, up ending ornaments, tipping over candleholders. Lucy watched the linen hand-towel, on the end of the sideboard, the towel in which she had wrapped Tobie’s hair...

“Take this woman to the cell,” Marten commanded. “Take responsibility for her, Bolls. We’ll search this chamber thoroughly before we admit anyone. We must find the ring.” He glanced back at the couch, saying, “I’ll search the body.”

Lucy saw Ludwig brush the linen cloth to the floor before she found herself grasped on either side as Captain Bolls and a guard hauled her from the room.

Chapter Seventeen

Lucy's silent prayer was disrupted by many clamorous sounds as she was pulled, half-dragged, swiftly along the corridor and down a wide stairway. Sounds of combat: clashing swords, shouts and curses darted along various passages of the palace and up the staircase. The two guards, holding one forearm each, ignored the fracas. Having one destination in mind, they drew Lucy toward a narrow downward step-way.

The royal residence was in chaos, but Lucy's only concern was for the prince. She prayed he was out of danger, and was moving away from the ominous threat of his enemies.

A group of four soldiers and a captain blocked their way. "Prince Lothar, where is he?" the captain demanded.

"Dead, Sir, killed" the guard answered, releasing Lucy as he saluted.

"Dead! Where? Who killed him?"

"In his chamber, Sir. I don't know anything else, Sir..."

"He's not dead," Lucy said, "he's alive. But, Ludwig and the Chief Brigadier will kill him if they find out."

"She lies," her guard said, drawing his sword. "We've orders to take her downstairs. I'm in charge of this prisoner." Turning to Lucy, he commanded, "You will not speak. We will..."

But the other captain and his men drew their swords. Lucy's guard backed to the wall, his eyes on her. As the swords clashed, Lucy joined him, saying, "Prince—King—Lothar is alive! Please take me to the king's chambers. Please, if you would help your king..."

Lucy had no idea how her presence with the prince would help him, but her own instinct of self-preservation made her realize that the best way out of this confusion would be along the passage to the mausoleum; and the guard had revealed that its source was the king's chambers.

"This way," the guard ordered, beckoning Lucy to follow him. She shuddered, not sure that she should trust him.

They hurried back the way they had come, then ascended the wide stairway. Choosing the opposite direction to the prince's chambers, the guard stepped into a brilliantly lit, wide corridor. A soldier Lucy recognized, met them.

Lucy's guard reached for his sword.

"No!" Lucy cried. "He's loyal to the prince!"

The guard ignored her and slid his sword from its sheath. "Where is the prince?" her escort demanded of the soldier. "Let me run him through. I'll be promoted after I kill Lothar!" He deftly blocked the soldier's sword slash.

Sliding along the wall behind her escort and ducking his sword as he slashed at her, Lucy fled along the corridor to the wide double-doors at the end. Without hesitation, she entered. The prince was there, sitting in a chair with his head between his knees as if trying to avoid fainting. He looked up at the sound of the doors being opened. The one guard in the room allowed her to walk to the prince.

"Lucy..." He stood, but reeled, and both she and the guard hurried to support him. "I will not leave without you."

"He wouldn't go," the guard muttered grimly, "but we must hurry now."

"Yes," Lucy said, "There's a traitor right on our heels, a very skilled swordsman." She felt the prince sagging, leaning on her shoulder, and asked, "Is there somewhere we can hide?"

"There's only one hope: if we can get out from the mausoleum and go to the casern for help," the prince said, turning but still supporting himself on Lucy and the guard. "Help me through the king's bed-chamber."

Lucy felt a chill to know that the secret passage to the mausoleum had been built in the king's quarters. Shuddering, she moved along with the prince's unsteady walk.

"Here, let me do it," Lothar said, lifting his uninjured arm to press his palm on a shield embedded in the wall.

The guard snatched up a cresset torch as they entered the revealed secret passage.

"Help me, Wayne," the prince said. "There's a lever, there, and a chain, see it? No one can follow us if the lever is secured with the chain, unless they have a large company to break through the wall.

The trek along the secret passage was slow, down numerous steps, but Lucy was relieved that they were moving away from the murderers.

Lothar, with help from Wayne, caused the familiar rumble to happen and Lucy saw wall torches lighting the mausoleum. The guard, his sword extended, went first. "It'd be safer for you to wait here, Sire. We don't know what's waiting for us further on. I'll check that the way is clear and find some loyal men at the casern." He turned to Lucy, "Follow me up here, Miss, so you can bolt the door from this side.

He ascended the stairs, and Lucy followed, locking the door behind him as he requested. She wondered if they were doing the right thing in remaining in the mausoleum.

Prince Lothar leaned heavily on his mother's tomb, and then dropped to his knees, uttering incomprehensible words that ended in a moan. Lucy wished she could comfort him, but was inexperienced in such matters and felt helpless. Cowering away from him, she waited and hoped help would come soon.

"Lucretia, here. Help to me stand up."

Lucy shuddered at his command. She did not know him, did she? They were here, alone. The illusion in the orange torchlight was very real. "You...you are dressed like Tobie now, and you look like him. I can't come closer..." Lucy, confused with her own feelings, drew back as Lothar struggled from a kneeling position. He pulled himself to stand up. She felt small and lost, afraid to be near him, yet longing to help him.

Bowing his head, Lothar leaned against the tomb. "I trusted Ludwig." He struck his clenched fist in sorrow on the marble. Stepping across to where his father's unfinished tomb had been placed, he said, "Father was right! And I did not believe him!" His voice broke as he said, "I did not believe him..."

There was a silence, and then he spoke dejectedly, "Now it's too late!"

"It's not too late," Lucy contradicted, and she saw his body jerk as though with a spasm. *He forgot I was here,* she thought, *Wayne has been gone a while...I hope everything is all right.*

Reaching down the front of her torn, gray dress, Lucy untied the key at her waist. "We could go up through my father's tomb..."

"There's no key for that gate," Lothar said, though moving closer to see what she held.

"I have a key," she began, then gasped as she felt his arms moving slowly but firmly around her shoulders. She struggled.

In consternation and pain, he released her. "Lucy..." he spoke with tenderness. "Lucretia. Father said you might still be alive. He said Lucretia Melville could well be the Lucy we sought..." He stepped closer and apparently saw anxiety clouding her blue eyes. "Don't be afraid of me. I'm Lothar, not Tobie. And I wish to thank you, Lucretia, not harm you..."

"I...I fear you will not be able to escape...and...you must be thirsty..." She backed away and hurried to fetch her bag, remembering her flask of cider.

Thirstily downing several mouthfuls herself, she gave the flask to the prince, saying, “Sweet cider. It’s all I have to offer Your Highness.” Realizing she had drunk before him, she apologized. “I...I’ve not eaten today, and the cider will give us strength...” She waited while he emptied the flask.

They both started as the door above was banged upon. “Shall we unlock the gate?” Lucy asked, but the sound of feet descending into her father’s tomb answered before he could reply.

“We mustn’t unlock the gate. Come.” Reaching to grasp her hand firmly, Lothar surprised her by kissing it tenderly, and then drew her with him, speaking firmly, “Come with me quickly and do as I say!”

Releasing her, he then spoke gently, “I cannot—I will not—lose you now Lucy.” Snatching up a torch, he said, “Quick, come this way.” Lothar strode ahead.

Lucy knew soldiers were almost in the Melville tomb as the approaching footsteps grew louder. How long would the gate hold out against the men’s force? Perhaps only minutes remained before the mausoleum was filled with those incensed that the prince was still alive. There was nothing she could do but follow Lothar, her small feet flying as she tried to keep his wavering torch in sight.

The jiggling of the gate, followed by louder rattling, spurred them on.

Chapter Eighteen

"I used to explore down here when my parents came to remember and pray. There were so many never-ending memorials to observe..." Lothar smiled down into Lucy's upturned face and, as though confessing a secret, said, "I was not an angel of a child and like any other, I liked to explore..." He extended the torch. "Ah, that small arch, there it is..."

Lothar bent low to pass under the arch, and Lucy, following, drew a breath as she saw this new chamber was as large as the one they had been in. She followed Lothar to the far end of the crypt, only to discover yet another chamber after ascending seven stone steps.

We are on our way up, she told herself, feeling heartened, then alarmed for a few seconds when she could not see the torch. The prince had moved behind a tall tomb, which Lucy stumbled against in the darkness. Groping around a cold marble effigy, she welcomed the orange flickers of light leading the way between the graves.

Lothar paused at the far corner of this long sepulcher to wait for Lucy. "I remember an aperture, up high, behind that statue." The prince stepped to the wall and swiftly climbed up into the recess, disappearing behind a larger-than-life effigy of a woman who, to Lucy, looked rather like the Madonna.

Stiffening as muffled echoes of swift footsteps pulsated in the musty air, Lothar dropped the torch and rolled it under his sandaled foot, extinguishing the smoking flame. Placing the stave end of the torch under his injured armpit, he reached down, commanding softly, "Take my hand."

Donning her carry-bag, and pushing it to her back, Lucy was swung up behind the tall statue. Lothar, using his good arm, pulled himself into a recess above the statue.

"Take my hand!" he ordered again. She obeyed and they quickly stood together on a narrow ledge.

"Hold tight here," the prince whispered, drawing her trembling fingers up to a corner piece of marble projecting from the wall. Feeling for a higher ledge, Lothar then disappeared even further above her. Ready for him this time, she held up her hand and was lifted to where he crouched. He drew her close, and then pulled her up to stand next to him.

He whispered again, drawing her even nearer, "We must be still, or we'll betray our hiding place."

Trembling uncontrollably, Lucy held her breath as Lothar, his arm encircling her small waist, tightened his hold. Ominous approaching footsteps blended with her racing heartbeat and, as she closed her eyes and leaned her head on Lothar's chest, she was sure *his* thudding heart was loud enough for all to hear. Boots moved in every direction and thunderous echoes encircled the concealed couple. Suddenly, the pounding reverberated immediately beneath them.

A shrill male voice caused Lucy to jump, "They're not here, Sir!"

An answering voice, "They *must* be here! Someone came along that passage, and it wasn't a ghost who bolted the doors! They have to be here!"

More boots, another deep voice, "No sign of either Tobie or the girl in the passage, Sir."

Stillness pervaded the area while the men stood to attention, waiting. Wavering slightly, a faint glow rose up the shaft beneath the couple.

A pair of boots sounded out below them and Marten's voice resonated, loud and clear, "How on earth can she have disappeared with a body? Tobie was definitely dead! I saw to it myself! It's impossible! Search every inch of this place! Take your time. We'll work our way back to the doors." His boots shuffled, one after the other; and others joined the chorus. Both Lothar and Lucy imagined that one or two men had climbed behind the large statue.

Marten demanded, “Here, give me that torch!”

“I’ve looked there, Sir. She could not climb, Sir, not with a body!”

The fugitives exhaled together, both comforted somewhat to know the clothes switch had fooled their enemies. At least, for the moment.

Feeling strangely safe, Lucy leaned still nearer Lothar, seeking to draw strength and comfort from him. They both softly inhaled again as the light grew brighter, passing right beneath them. Lucy, feeling she would scream, bit her lip hard.

Darkness returned suddenly to the hiding place as they heard Marten jump from the level of the shrine to the floor. Lucy felt Lothar relax and release his breath and she did the same, only to catch it again at the sound of approaching footsteps and Ludwig’s questioning voice.

“Where is she?” he demanded. “There’s no way out! To where has she disappeared? How did she know the way into the passage? What did she do with Tobie?” No answers were offered. “There’s no way out of here that we do not have covered. She has to be in here, hiding somewhere. Start searching again but do it more thoroughly. Perhaps some of the lids on the graves can be lifted. She may be hiding in one of the tombs. Try them all.”

Footsteps, grunts, and moving lights signaled renewed activity. The light dimmed, but still glowed faintly as the search moved into the other chambers. Lucy and Lothar remained as still as they could. The search seemed to go on forever.

The light became bright again as Ludwig extended his torch behind the statue, straining his eyes, trying to seek out what lay in the dark recess that so obviously stretched above. He laughed, and it was a chilling sound.

His voice, filled with satisfaction and triumph, was a little breathless, as he said, “Perhaps she’s a witch and she’s *disappeared* with Tobie. Perhaps the guard spoke truly and Tobie *was* standing up as though alive in the king’s chambers. And now, she’s returned from whence she came. At least she saved us from being labeled as murderers. The deed is done. What these catacombs conceal, must remain concealed."

Ludwig stared up at the statue, silent and still for a minute before concluding, "I want a constant guard on this place, as of now."

Marten said, "Come Sire, we must take the prince to lie with his father, and we must make preparations for his tomb. It will be a sad funeral for the kingdom, that of a king and his son, the last of a line. But, great things lie in store for those who are obedient to the new rule!"

Ludwig's eyes lingered on the statue's rigid face. "Such a pity. She was very beautiful. We could have done great things. At least Lothar did not win her..."

Lothar's grip on Lucy tightened as Ludwig continued, his ominous whisper floating up the shaft, "I may find my virgin princess yet."
A breathless guard arrived, saluting Marten. "You must come, Sir; both of you. The doctor...the embalmer..."

"What is it?" Marten commanded. "Tell us."

"The body, Prince Lothar. They did not find the ring, Sir. You and Sir Ludwig must come. There is a problem, but the doctor must tell you."

"What next?" Ludwig asked.

Marten strode away with Ludwig following, the torch-bearing soldiers marching behind them.

Lucy shivered as the echoing footsteps grew fainter. Neither she nor Lothar moved until the silence and darkness were complete. Then, very slowly, but surely, Lothar's hand moved from Lucy's shoulder and gently caressed the back of her neck. Moving upward to her hair, his fingers walked around her braids before lingering lightly on her temple. Stroking her forehead with the backs of his fingers, he bent to kiss the same place. Lucy did not move, but waited tensely until the prince's hand moved back across her neck to her shoulder. She shuddered, but felt strangely comforted and safe.

Intending to ask how they would escape from here, Lucy stammered, “How will? They will guard...and watch for us.”

Lothar, sliding his right hand down her arm, entwined his smooth lean fingers in hers, saying, “We’ll climb further. There’s a small channel, square, I recall, and after shifting an obstacle or two, we can exit. At least, I used to when I was a boy. It caused my mother to swoon when she heard that I was missing in the mausoleum. Then I mysteriously turned up, out on the street. They thought I had somehow evaded the guard and climbed the steps. I hope the channel is not too small for me now.”

To Lucy, the passage ahead was black nothingness. Instinctively clinging to him, she allowed Lothar to direct her movements as they continued up the shaft.

“The exit is between the mausoleum wall and the city wall; a little above ground level,” Lothar said before crawling into the dark channel that led to the outside. “I’ve no idea why it was formed, except that some predecessor may have believed air should be allowed to escape from beneath. I don’t think the shaft is referred to in any drawings or records of the mausoleum.”

He helped Lucy into the opening. Without wording the fact, both knew they were far above the mausoleum floor, and slipping or losing hold now would mean a plunge to certain death.

Lucy was relieved as the channel became horizontal. They were crawling towards the outside, and she kept reaching one hand forward for a reassuring touch of Lothar’s sandals. The passage narrowed and Lucy wondered if the prince would be able to keep wriggling along the restrictive path.

Soon he came to a halt. Grunting at the added strain he placed on his injured arm, Lothar began to push with all his might, using both hands. Lucy wondered what he was struggling with, but waited patiently. She could not help him as the channel was just large enough for one. Finally, he gave up, exhaling loudly, obviously frustrated.

“What is it?” Lucy asked, knowing full well that something was blocking the way.

“It’s like a miniature portcullis, an upright gridiron. The metal bars are closer together than I remembered. When I was a boy, I managed to push it up and hold it there until I crawled through.” He took several deep breaths before resuming normal breathing. “It falls back into its place when released. But it won’t budge!”

He used the torch-stave as a lever and the bars shifted a little. With more pressure on the strong stave, the grate lifted from its slots and dropped back as Lothar released the leverage. Using his hands again, he raised the grate easily, saying, “There, that’s almost like it used to be. It’s become stiff from lack of use.” Turning to Lucy, he said with a smile, “There’ve been no young explorers up here lately.”

Lothar propped the mini portcullis up with the stave and warned, “Take care, you must not knock the stave. It’s on your right.”

Lucy wriggled forward cautiously, moving as far to the left as she could. She had drawn her skirts up and held the fabric between her teeth. Clenching her jaw tightly helped quench her rising panic. This small, close channel made her feel entombed. Her carry-bag rolled to her left side, and she pushed it firmly to her back. However, as she moved under the grill, the bag slid to her right side, knocking against the stave, causing it to shift forward. Dreading what might happen, Lucy pushed with her left knee, hoping to propel herself clear of the frame if it fell.

A portcullis has spikes on the bottom, she thought, and, having dragged her right leg under her body, she realized the unthinkable had happened. She was trapped, unable to move. She felt nothing for a second, and then intense pain shot up her left leg, causing her to release the fabric from her mouth as she emitted a strangled cry. She collapsed in shock, her right knee knocking the air out of her body.

Contorting from the paining, as though it might somehow release her, she twisted her free leg sideways to lie flat on the stone-lined channel floor. The movement, however, caused the grill to settle even more, pinning her left leg completely.

Struggling now with an odd-shaped stone, Lothar was unaware of Lucy's dilemma.

With a fierce shove, the prince finally moved the stone. Pivoting on a metal rod through a knob-like protrusion, the stone turned outwards, and fresh early-evening air rushed into the chamber. Lothar did not speak as he climbed from the channel and surveyed the area, listening for any sound of life.

"Come, quick! The way is clear," Lothar called, crouching so his head was level with the opening.

"I can't!" Lucy called back, unable to prevent a sob, her voice strained.

Frowning, Lothar waited a few seconds, and then he climbed back into the channel headfirst.

Lucy lay with her hot cheek upon the cool stone of the chamber, thinking, *I'm stuck here...it surely will be my tomb.* She raised her head as she felt Lothar's hand contact her shoulder.

"You'll...have...to...go...without me," Lucy tried to keep her voice steady. "You...must find loyal men...somewhere...out there."

Lothar was confused as he tried to fathom her reasoning, "We won't stay here. Come!" He reached under Lucy's armpit, trying to drag her forward. At her wounded cry, his tugging ceased.

"What is it?" Lothar asked, but knew even before she answered, and a feeling of dread came over him.

"The stave...must have fallen...the grate...is on my leg," Lucy said, then in a pained whimper she begged, "Please go...please..."

"Where on your leg?" Lothar asked. Mustering his composure, he added a second question, "The spikes, did one...?" His hand trembled to feel Lucy's shoulders rising and falling as she broke into uncontrollable sobs. Cradling her head with his right arm, and caressing her hair with his left, Lothar waited several minutes until her cries diminished. Forgetting the threat of being heard and found, he asked again about the spikes and the position of the grate on her leg.

"It's above my ankle, on my calf." Lucy said. "I...I...don't think...the spike isn't through my leg...it's...at the side." She moaned and added, "I can't move my leg...it's pinned by the weight of the bar."

Raising himself and moving away from her face, Lothar said, "You must be released!" He knew if the spike had cut her leg, she might bleed to death. Time was precious.

"No!" Lucy cried, reaching out for him. She grasped the shoulders of Tobie's tunic, using both hands. "No...please...don't leave me!" The exertion to hold Lothar caused beads of perspiration to glimmer on her brow, but she mustered all her energy, believing that holding on to him would save *his* life.

Lothar attempted to pry Lucy's hands from the tunic. "I must go. Release me, Lucy!" Lothar's voice was strained as he then said firmly, "I command that you let go of me!"

Lucy's imagination was filled with pictures of Lothar entering the mausoleum, the many guards preventing him, cutting him down with their sharp swords, stabbing him with their daggers. Her grip became tighter and she sobbed in anguish and grief. Suddenly, he was all she needed for comfort and care. And love. How lonely she had been all her life without him.

The prince was still. Recognizing her deep distress, he was waiting for her to tire and release him. When she continued holding him, he relaxed and wriggled forward so that their heads were level. Caressing her hair and wiping the tears with the backs of his fingers, he felt her grip slacken.

"You said you could not lose me...now." She said in his ear, her sobs subsiding as she released one hand from the fabric of the tunic and touched his cheek gently. "I...I do not...want...to lose you."

Carefully, he twisted so they were face to face, and his lips found hers in a tender kiss. The prince kissed the tears on her cheeks, and felt the whisper of a sigh escape her lips. She was trembling, and her energy was spent.

"We shall not lose each other. Not now!" Lothar said with determination, his tone very gentle. He kissed her, gently, again and again, until she ceased trembling and relaxed.

"I must raise the gridiron," he said firmly, backing swiftly away.

"No!" Lucy stretched out her hand, but he was out of reach. "Wait!" She thought of her carry bag, and said, "I have...a gray wig. You won't be recognized...if you wear it."

The prince stayed outside Lucy's reach for a moment, but crawled back to assist when he heard her soft moans as she struggled with the straps of her carry-bag. Once the bag was free, she reached inside and felt for the wig. Drawing it from the bag, she allowed Lothar to take the hairpiece.

"Please don't enter the mausoleum again. They'll kill you. I could not live if...if something happens to you," Lucy said as he backed from the channel.

"We will see. Perhaps it will be best to fetch help..." Lothar said, and then added as if to comfort her, "You're right. We need help. If I try to enter the mausoleum and am captured, they'll guess you're here somewhere. There are loyal Christian men in Lotharingia, and I'll find them."

Moving back to her, Lothar kissed her again, slowly, and with tender passion, then he was gone.

For a moment, Lucy saw faint light entering the channel as Lothar stepped from the entrance, allowing the rising moon to shine in. Darkness prevailed again after Lothar swung the stone back into the opening.

Chapter Nineteen

Prince Lothar crept around the mausoleum, pressing himself against the heavy stonewall, moving stealthily toward the entrance. Peering around a corner, he saw the backs of soldiers, silhouetted by the light of the rising moon. They stood with swords drawn, and Lothar knew they had been commanded to watch diligently for Lucy. He wondered where they thought she would come from, but then realized their attention was upon the entrance to Lord Melville's tomb. They expected her to attempt an escape from there.

Returning past the closed channel and circumnavigating the mausoleum to view the entrance to the royal mausoleum, Lothar was startled to hear a voice calling "Halt! Who goes there?" Then, "Quick, it could be the girl!"

Pulling the wig over his head as he ran along the alley away from the mausoleum, Lothar brushed the fuzzy gray hair from his eyes and straightened the back of it. Voices, calling, broke the stillness of the evening, and Lothar heard horses' hooves pounding the path behind him. They would surely capture him!

Somewhat familiar with the area, Lothar knew he was not far from the smaller city gates. However, he needed to lose his pursuers. Diving up a narrow alley, he crouched behind a high stone step-way, waiting for the horses to pass on.

I must rally the loyal militia of Lotharingia, he thought, *but how do I do this? Marten is in charge, and his orders will be obeyed, unless I prove my identity.* He felt for the seal ring he wore on the middle finger of his right hand. *At least Ludwig did not steal this from me...but he would have once he had my body in his grasp...* Lothar knew that this ring would be the most important object Ludwig would want to gain when he realized it was Tobie's body at the palace. Lothar frowned as his thoughts returned to Lucy and her pain, and he stood, knowing he must gain help as quickly as possible.

The two steel-braced wooden gates were closed. Two guards monitored a narrow door within one gate. Lothar was thankful for the gray wig, because he was sure guards on the gates would be in the pay of Ludwig.

"Are y' on y' own?" one guard asked. Before Lothar could reply, he added, "Y' haven't seen a widda womin, or a girl, have y'?"

"I'm walking out to the Melville," Lothar said, looking back at the dark streets. He added, "there's no womin here."

The prince was relieved when the men did not question him further and allowed him to pass. As he broke into a light jog, he nursed his sore arm with his right hand. Progressing hardly a hundred yards, he heard the gate behind swing open. Two horses, each carrying a palace guard, cantered past him.

Marten will be calling in all available cavalry...he'll be issuing orders so that the kingdom will be secured for Ludwig. He'll likely say that Prince Lothar is dead and when he discovers Tobie in my place, he'll still announce that I'm dead. The traitor will be buried in my place. Marten will do all in his power to see me dead. It'll be difficult for me to prove who I am without being slain for high treason.

With each step he took, Lothar reminded himself of Marten and Ludwig's treachery; it made victory against them seem impossible. *Our Chief Brigadier, a traitor working against the throne with my trusted companion, Ludwig. Who else will welcome their evil schemes?*

Lothar determined not to reveal himself until had he gained the safety of the Melville. *Brother Daniel and Father Francis will give me sanctuary and advice*—Lothar counted on this as he had no idea who else was loyal.

The mile to the Melville seemed forever and Lothar, trying to imagine what Ludwig and Marten were planning, was not surprised to hear a company riding out from the Melville. The horses' hooves pounded loudly in the still night air.

Moving off the road as the company approached, Lothar bowed his head so the moonlight was not on his face. However, Leo and the two other soldiers at Tobie's capture at Melville Castle were present in the company. They recognized Tobie's clothing and saw the wig for what it was.

"Whoa!" Leo pulled his horse to a halt and sprang from the saddle. Drawing his sword, he demanded, "Who are you? Name yourself!" Leo was swiftly joined by his two companions. Others at the tail of the cavalcade reined their horses around to view the confrontation. Many had known Tobie as night watchman at the Melville Gate, and they saw only the murderous traitor now.

Quick-witted enough to realize the soldier's intentions, Lothar snatched the wig from his head, exclaiming, "I am Lothar, king of Lotharingia, and I seek men who are loyal to the throne!" As the swords drew nearer, he saw incredulity and disbelief on their faces. Holding the gold seal ring up to the moonlight, he cried, "I'm unarmed. This is the king's ring, and for the sake of Lotharingia, I command your fidelity!" He stood his ground, waiting for them to lower their swords, knowing the other soldiers were riding back towards the three.

"You must watch! The troops are divided," Lothar warned, "the palace is in Ludwig's control. Chief Brigadier Marten is plotting against the throne. He attempted to kill me and thinks I am dead, but..." Lothar, not wishing to take the time to explain how he was in the traitors clothes, searched for a way to prove his title and claim. An approaching horseman wearing black trousers of the Palace Guards, leapt from his saddle, and Lothar was sure the man recognized him.

"Look out, behind you," he warned, "defend yourselves!"

"The prince!" the disloyal guard exclaimed, drawing his sword and advancing. "It's Lothar, the Prince! He's alive, but won't remain so!"

The area was a battleground for several minutes before the two palace guards and one other lay dead. Sheathing his bloodstained sword, Leo spoke grimly, "We'll return to the Melville and sort this out." He was not convinced of the prince's identity, but he knew this man's face, voice, and manner were not Tobie's.

How can this be Tobie? Tobie's dead! The palace guards killed him. There was an attempt on the prince's life, and then came a report that the prince was dead and we were needed to guard the palace against an uprising...

"Ride with me," he offered gruffly, then added, "Your Highness." Watching the prince mount awkwardly due to his injury, Leo then swung himself up behind. "There is treachery at the palace, Captain Emil! Those loyal to King Lothar must return and secure the Melville."

To himself, he thought, *I hope he* is *the King's son. If not, I'll be executed for treason!*

Captain Emil, seeing that the two men who had come to summon them to the palace were now dead, chose to follow Leo, knowing the young man to be very loyal.

"Leave the bodies and return to the Melville," Emil commanded.

***

Lothar addressed an expanding group of men assembling in the castle foyer on Brother Daniel's side of the Melville, explaining how Ludwig and Marten were seeking to seize the throne.

"Such a reign will only bring terror and injustice to the Lotharingian people," Lothar explained.

Father Francis arrived with a group of men from his side.

Brother Daniel said, "We have no doubts that this man is Lothar. Every loyal person believing in the freedom of the Christian faith should take up arms and fight for their—our— country and rid it of the evil that could engulf and destroy us all."

"We'll rally the loyal troops," Captain Emil announced, his voice trembling. Such a crisis was unexpected, unprecedented! He looked around at the small company. "We'll have to divide to spread the word." He turned to Lothar. "We'll need documents sealed with the king's ring. I'm glad you still have your rings, Sire!"

Lothar tried to keep his thoughts from Lucy's predicament as he took up a sword. "Captain Emil, as of this moment, you are the Chief Brigadier of Lotharingia and commander of all our armies."

Emil, overcome, stared at the prince for several seconds before dropping to his knees and swearing his loyalty.

Lightly touching Emil's shoulders with the sword, Lothar commanded, "Rise, Sir Emil, Chief Brigadier of the armies of Lotharingia." He held his hand to Emil, who kissed the seal ring.

"Kneel, Leo," he said, turning.

Leo knelt quickly. "Leonhard, at your service, Sire. I swear to you my life, and to fight for justice and the Christian faith for the good of Lotharingia."

Solemnly touching the sword to Leo's shoulders, Lothar said, "Rise, Sir Leonhard, Second Brigadier of the armies of Lotharingia."

Again, the ring was kissed.

Lothar then commanded, "Come, we have a perilous mission before we can summon the troops and take the palace." He studied their solemn faces.

"Sire, it would be safer for you to remain at the Melville," Emil told him. "You're weak from your wound. We'll summon the troops and have them rendezvous here, but you must remain. The kingdom cannot afford to lose its king." He judiciously omitted the words, *and you have no heir.*

Lothar moved toward the chaplain's office, wishing he could stop time. "Come, we'll counsel. Bring the two chaplains, and six of your wisest and most loyal men."

His heart felt like a stone as he pictured Lucy alone with her pain. He wasn't afraid her being discovered—her hiding place was secure—but he was anxious about her injury.

In the office, he condensed the account, and in minutes told about the dagger in the throne room, how Lucretia Melville disguised as a widow woman had saved his life by her well-timed scream. He then told of her bravery under extremely negative tensions, how she had fooled Marten by the exchange of clothes, their escape to the mausoleum, and Lucy's subsequent accident with the gridiron.

"I earnestly petition your assistance to rescue Lady Melville." Lothar saw the disagreement upon their faces, and thought it was because he was placing Lucy before the immediate needs of the kingdom. "We must go, with those who will help us."

He turned to Brother Daniel and said, "We covet the prayers of all who remain here..." His eyes included Father Francis. "We must make haste..."

Emil voiced their fears: "If Marten wants you dead Sire, he will stop at nothing. When he finds Tobie in your place and he believes you are still alive, he'll be furious..." He saw the set of Lothar's face and bowed, saying, "We waste precious time! Come, we will rescue the young lady."

"It's the Queen of Lotharingia we go to rescue, for I will marry Lucretia as soon as the vigil for my father is over," Prince Lothar said decisively.

***

Gathering every available sword-hand and leaving a few to secure the Melville, a company of thirty-four galloped from the fortress.

Lothar now wore a captain's uniform and there was no doubt to any who saw him, that this was the prince, the heir to the throne, the king-to-be-crowned.

Lothar hoped, and prayed, that the guard on the mausoleum had abandoned their post without finding Lucy and that they had not discovered that he was still alive...

Chapter Twenty

The company was permitted to ride through the city gates after Emil declared, truthfully, that they had been summoned from the Melville. The new Chief Brigadier would like to have gained control of the gates, but he knew this might backfire and Marten could become aware of trouble. He must obey the king's directive to rescue Lucy first.

Choosing the narrow road beside the wall, Lothar led the way. Two hours had passed, and he was increasingly anxious. As they neared the mausoleum, his heart leapt within his chest, almost snatching his breath away. Smoke in the shape of two large funnels roared from the two entrances, mushrooming into dense clouds, drawn from the ground by an updraft. Choking black fumes issued from cracks in the stone roof of the underground edifice.

"They've set fire to the royal mausoleum!" Emil exclaimed. He drew his horse alongside, seeking Lothar's reaction.

The royal mausoleum was, indeed, an inferno! The guards, so intent upon watching the two exits, did not see, nor hear, the now cautious approach of the prince and his company.

"No, Sire!" Emil shouted over the din. But the prince forced his mount forward across the cobblestones. The horse, obedient until it felt the heat from the flames, whinnied and shied until the prince brought it under control, riding closer still. Dismounting, Lothar ran toward the entrance.

Realizing the prince's blind intention, the men followed, charging their horses in pursuit. Then, leaping from their mounts, they raced to create a blockade between the prince and the guards to prevent them apprehending or fighting their sovereign.

Coughing and spluttering, Emil and Leo dragged Lothar away from the steps, out of the choking fumes. He fought them, but they held tight, and his strength waned as his injured arm caused pain enough to match his internal anguish.

A muffled explosion shook the ground, and every man and horse withdrew further back from the mausoleum.

"More marble will explode if it gets any hotter," Emil said, as they pulled the prince even further away after the explosion.

The ear-shattering boom was still reverberating when several more resounded. Some horses shied, while others bolted. A close guard formed around the prince but all attention was upon the building as if everyone expected the whole place to erupt like a volcano.

"You mustn't approach Sire—it's suicide!" Emil looked into the prince's stricken eyes and his tone softened. "We can do nothing, Sire, it's impossible."

Lothar sagged against the arms holding him firmly, saying, "Release me." He dropped to his knees, his mind blank. There were no more explosions. All was silent. Strangely, the fire had abruptly burned itself out.

The prince prayed, *Please, God, please, God. You can work miracles...* He turned his face to stare at the full moon now showing its opaque glow through the smoke. *Lucy is gone, it should have been me.* His thoughts replied, *But I did not die when they tried to kill me. How do I know she's dead? Have I seen her body?*

Taking Leo's arm, he pulled himself to his feet. "She's not dead! I can't—I won't—believe it until I see her body." His eyes locked with Emil's. "I won't try to go in there, but we'll go around to the vent..." He closed his eyes, knowing if Lucy was still where he left her, she was, indeed, dead. The black smoke would have smothered her, choked her. He shuddered at the feel of Emil's sympathetic hand upon his shoulder.

"We'll wait awhile longer, then go and retrieve her body," Emil said, and they turned, watching the smoke disperse.

The moon seemed to move across the sky as the smoke quickly thinned. Stillness pervaded the area, and the men stood like cemetery statues.

"We'll kill everyone involved in this, Your Majesty, you can count on that," Leo hissed in Lothar's ear, offering his words as condolence to the young monarch, who had tears trickling down his cheek.

Lothar slowly turned to Leo and said, "Revenge is the worst of pastimes, for it never brings satisfaction, nor happiness. No, we won't seek revenge. We'll keep our memories pure and not soil purity with bitterness." He stared at the moon for several minutes, and then spoke with resignation, "We must accept the inevitable. The Lord gives and the Lord takes away..." He paused and whispered, "Blessed be the Name of the Lord."

Then, feeling as though his heart had numbed, Lothar spoke in an automatic mode, "We must consider Lotharingia. We should speak to the men."

The guard around him moved back, and Lothar approached the twenty or so outnumbered men. They stood to attention, swords drawn. The prince looked into their faces one by one, and said, "The king of Lotharingia is not dead. You see him here in the flesh, together with the seal ring." He held up his right hand and asked, "Will you offer your fealty?"

As most of the soldiers sheathed their swords and dropped to kneel, one asked, "I've not seen Lothar, except from afar. You could be anyone. How do we know you're him?" Alarm swiftly crossed his face as those around the prince moved toward him with aggression.

"Stand your ground!" Lothar commanded, raising his hand. He turned to the young soldier. "What is your name?"

"Rex of Southwood."

"You're right to question my claim, Rex. I *could* be a traitor, and a traitor *did* try to steal my ring recently. But I am Lothar, son of the late king, and I assure you this ring is mine. Tell me, do you believe in God?

"Yes, of course."

"*Which* god?

Rex frowned, then answered, "The One True God."

"Who is the One True God? Describe him."

"The God of Heaven; the Creator of the Heavens and Earth..."

"Have you seen him?"

"No. No one has seen God. Those who believe, see Him through faith..." Rex's voice tapered to a whisper as he perceived his words in the light of his challenge, and he knelt and bowed his head with humility..

Lothar verbalized Rex's thoughts, "Then you must likewise believe that I am the king-elect, whom you have not seen close up. I also believe in the One True God; and we must earnestly pray for His help and strength if we are to thwart His enemies."

Lothar turned to the men, "We must unite to save our kingdom from those who are planning to kill every person refusing to denounce the Christian faith, that God is the Father of our Lord Jesus Christ, and that He is King of Kings. These people are lead by Marten and Ludwig who sought to secure my throne for themselves. But God's intervention has interrupted their murderous plans!"

"God bless the King!" Emil called, and the others joined the cry, "God save Lotharingia! God bless King Lothar!"

The smoke, now a lazy smolder, began to fade. The prince looked toward the mausoleum. "How did this arson happen?" He swept the twenty kneeling guards. "What part did you play in it?"

"We had orders from Sir Marten to capture anyone escaping from the mausoleum, Sire," the captain answered. Standing, he bowed, saluted, and continued, "Captain Trent, your humble servant. I was told that a woman, and perhaps a man—a criminal—was down there. We were to capture the woman, kill the man, and then take both to the palace..."

"You knew nothing about the conspiracy?" Emil stepped closer to the captain.

"No." Captain Trent replied. "Like all diligent captains, we do not ask questions, we follow orders!"

"How was the fire started?" Emil asked.

"Some men brought barrels of oil and poured them on the floor. They added rags—two carts of old rags were brought— then they were set alight. We were ordered to remain on guard and, when the fire died down, report to the palace."

"Marten and Ludwig obviously discovered that you are still alive, Your Majesty," Emil said.

Trent bowed his head. "Your Highness, forgive us. It was reported that you were dead. We believed it to be true. You must give us our next orders, Sire!"

The remaining smoke caught in the soft upward night breeze, but the glow and heat left no doubt that the mausoleum would still be unsafe to enter.

Lothar thought again of the channel. "The vent! Maybe...but, come, we must try," he said. "You men remain here and guard. Sir Emil, Sir Leonhard, Captain Trent, and Rex, yes, come with us."

Emil issued orders for the men to round up the remaining horses. As he helped Lothar mount, he offered words to prepare the prince for the disappointment that surely awaited him "No one could escape that inferno, it is impossible..."

The company followed the prince around the perimeter of the mausoleum, riding between the two walls. Smoke lingered in this alley, but again, the up draught drew it away as it seeped from the cracks around the stone blocking the vent.

Leo jumped from his horse simultaneously with Lothar, who rushed into the smoke wafting from the wall, his eyes set on the stone that destroyed all his hopes.

I have failed my love. I failed her, he thought desolately. *All hope is gone.* His fingers clawed at the stone. He had expected it to be hot, but it was only warm. He waved his hand at the smoke as he drew the stone around, coughing at the rush of black fumes.

"You cannot...you must not...go in there, Sire." Leo pulled Lothar, unresisting, from the smoke.

The prince's strength was spent. Leo and Emil supported their sovereign while he gave way to his deep despair.

Without hesitating, they put their arms around him and wept with him.

Lucy was my one and only love; a love that was given no time to grow. I will never love again, he told himself, *I will never love again...*

Chapter Twenty-one

Emil, ducking beneath the pall of smoke still pouring from the shaft, snatched up a carry-bag. Turning, he called, "Rex, the guards at the front had torches, fetch one." Speaking now to Lothar, he said, "Sire, you must come away now, the wind is uncertain, and this smoke is unhealthy. Come."

With Leo's help, he drew the prince aside.

They watched the smoke as if it were a funeral bier.

At the sight of the approaching torch, Emil dropped the bag to the ground. "Who would have left this here?" he asked, on one knee and undoing the fastenings.

Lothar continued to stare at the vent, but as the torch came closer, his attention moved lifelessly with the flame. Both nauseous and grief-stricken to think of Lucy, he winced at the memory of their kiss. How she had responded to him... She said she could not lose him. *But I have lost her, now, she is gone...* Tears seeped down his cheeks.

"Bring the torch closer," Emil commanded, opening the bag as the light fell across it.

Lothar drew a deep breath, suddenly realizing the importance of Emil's discovery. "That bag, it's Lucy's! But how did she...how *could* she...where...where can she be?" His voice was strained, as if not allowing himself to imagine she still lived. Pivoting his body, his eyes searched the immediate area. He stared back at the open vent and exclaimed, "The bag could not be out here unless...unless she managed to free herself, and push the stone out. But, why leave her bag?"

New hope overpowered him, but it was like a knot in his throat, threatening to choke him. He said, "We must find her. She can't have gone far. Oh, please, God, I pray she wasn't captured..."

Drawing Emil aside from the others, Lothar spoke softly, commanding, "Search the area, but put two of our men with each of

Trent's guards, just in case they turn. Tell them to be diligent. We must not lose her now. She'd be valuable to a traitor. Marten would give much for such a hostage."

"I'll organize a search. Leo, Trent, Rex, stay with His Majesty," Emil commanded, mounted his horse, and rode back around the mausoleum.

Leo took the torch from Rex, and commanded, "We're looking for Lady Lucretia Melville. She's injured, and can't have gone far. Spread out, search the area around the mausoleum." He held the torch close to the cobblestones beneath and dropped to one knee at the sight of a smear of blood.

Lothar knelt beside Leo, and then they wordlessly followed the faint trail around the building and along the wall to where tall weeds, growing in the hard earth, had been crushed and flattened. "She must have been here. The explosions would have frightened her, and, perhaps, she found somewhere to hide," Leo suggested, knowing the prince was hopeful that Lucy had not been captured. "Let's go back around the front and join the search from there."

At the front, Emil reported to the apprehensive prince. The company had searched, but so far there had been no sightings of Lucy. "There are crowds of people outside the palace, they would have heard the noise and seen the fire. The palace guards are not allowing anyone past the palace, and there are guards just up over the rise, here. We don't think Lady Melville went that way." Emil would have added, *unless she was captured,* but he thought better of it.

"We searched all back streets that were thoroughfares; we rode almost as far as the square. We've not had time to search every lane, but we did not see the maid..."

Lothar interrupted Emil, exclaiming, "She won't look like a maid! Did you see a woman dressed as a widow? Her gray dress was torn..." The question went unanswered as they turned synchronously at the sound of approaching horses.

A soldier raced breathlessly down the rise to stand before Lothar. "Your Majesty! Guards are riding...from the palace...they will want to know the results of the fire...they'll be wondering why we've not reported in."

"How many?" Lothar asked.

"Ten, maybe a dozen."

Lothar's eyes scanned the area around the mausoleum. "Rally our men, Emil!"

The guards rode down the gradient towards the mausoleum, two by two. Emil commanded his men into defensive positions. Eight, designated by Emil and Leo, flicked the safety clips from their crossbows and stood near the prince.

The new arrivals did not dismount, but lined their horses across the cobbled rectangle; obviously taking in the number of confronters and the fact that several of them wore civilian clothes. The leader spurred his horse forward.

"I am Captain Arnan, on orders from Sir Marten, the Chief Brigadier." His face was a mixture of authority and fear. His men were out-numbered and facing crossbows, which were intended for battle against *other* kingdoms, not against their own! "Bows and bolts? On whose authority do you confront us?"

Emil would have stepped forward, but Lothar placed his hand on the man's arm, and spoke. "I am Lothar, king of Lotharingia." He signaled a warning for his men to hold their fire. "Marten has committed treason against the throne of Lotharingia, which by right of succession, is my throne. Marten is no longer leader of my armies, and all who follow him are insubordinate. Dismount and surrender your swords and your lives will be spared."

He pivoted to introduce Emil as chief brigadier, but the mounted captain turned his horse before springing from it. Shielded by the animal, he drew his sword. Maneuvering the horse for protection, he started towards Lothar.

Emil and Leo did not wait. With swords drawn, they moved around the back of the horse, dragging it away so that Captain Arnan was exposed.

Men released their bolts whilst others raced to attack the mounted guards.

Not one of Marten's men indicated surrender, but several attempted to escape when the area became a battleground.

Soon, however, Captain Arnan and his men lay dead on the cobblestones, save one, who rode up the hill. A crossbowman reloaded quickly and took aim at the fleeing man.

"No! Let him go!" Lothar commanded.

The man obeyed, lowering the bow.

"Sire?" Emil questioned, confused.

"Ludwig and Marten's plans depend upon my being dead. Once they know I'm alive, they'll vacate the palace and leave the kingdom."

"But that man will report we are less than sixty. We must make haste to the Melville! If Marten comes here with two or three hundred, we're finished," Leo said.

The other men knew this was true. Sir Marten would be obeyed until the truth was known, and his hoards could easily wipe the small band out.

"We'll ride to the Melville," Lothar conceded.

Rex spoke, "Your Majesty, we need documents, signed by you, to present to all captains. If we all bear documents sealed with your ring, we could ride out all over the kingdom..."

There was hearty agreement to Rex's idea.

Lothar was disheartened and weary as he mounted his horse. His emotions had been first crushed and then revived. He had hoped to find Lucy, but he must now believe she had a place of refuge and would find help. He shuddered as he remembered the key and her bag, and that she had previously found shelter in the mausoleum.

She would not—could not— return there now.

And neither could he. It would not be safe in the city for them until Ludwig and Marten had been removed.

Where and when would they find each other again?

There is nothing else I can do, Lothar thought, reining his horse around, listening as Emil commanded the men to collect the weapons from the bodies and gather their horses, telling those who could not find mounts to ride tandem.

Emil voiced the prince's thoughts, "We cannot help Lady Melville until we rally the troops, Sire."

They spurred their horses into action, retracing the route back to the gates.

Chapter Twenty-two

After Lothar kissed her and left, Lucy had cradled her head sideways on her arm, and prayed; supplicating for Lothar, for his safety, for their country.

I love him, she told herself, feeling a new joy deep within her. Remembering her cousins and Cynthia, she prayed for their safety. Kingdom security was in a terrible state, and she felt sure Lord Tullus, his guards, and his footmen would join to help Lothar.

The once throbbing pain in her leg now felt dull, and Lucy realized it was numb. Raising herself to her elbows, she gingerly reached her free foot backwards and searched for a place to wedge her leather shoe. The toe of her shoe fit between the vertical bars above the thick bottom bar where the spikes slid into slots in the stone.

My leg may be broken, she thought, then felt relieved as the grill moved upwards from the firm pressure of her foot. The movement, however, brought pain to her injury. *I must ignore the pain. I must raise the grill and drag myself forward so it does not fall on my leg again.*

Concentrating, Lucy managed to raise the metal frame enough to free her leg. Propelling herself forward, she dragged her injured leg a few inches, gasping in pain as the frame fell, twisting and bruising her foot. The bar fastened onto her shoe and she expected sharper pain, but her foot was between the spikes. She repeated the lift with her right foot to release her shoe.

She was free! Collapsing to lie on the stone, she sobbed quietly, wishing that Lothar had not gone. How she longed to be with him now, to help him, to be in a safe place with him. Nothing meant more to her than Lothar's safety. *I will die if anything happens to him.* In a flash she realized how much she loved him. *Love is painful, yet sweet,* she mused. No one had ever affected her heart like him. Up until recently, all men had belonged in a place similar to the mausoleum. But now, she had fallen deeply in love with the king of Lotharingia!

So this is love, Lucy thought. *There is pain with love. My heart feels bruised with the thought that he is in danger. If only we could be together without fear, without threat... How wonderful it would be to come to know him more. This must be how he felt, when he saw me in the woods. If only...how I wish...* Lucy closed her mind to regret. *I am here, and in this predicament I must pray and believe God will help the prince.* I *can do nothing for him now.*

Expended, she relaxed and rested.

Ten minutes passed before Lucy remembered her freedom from the gridiron. Her dislike for this cramped stone vent circled her mind, and she remembered Lothar's danger again. She forced herself forward.

I must do all I can to help the prince, she thought, but ideas would not form in her tired mind.

Pushing her bag ahead, Lucy felt backwards for the stave. *It's the only thing I have to help me stand,* she reasoned as her fingers contacted the wood. Placing it with her bag, she moved the two together and gradually inched her way towards the opening. It was further than she imagined, and she longed to rest.

Oh, to bathe my aching leg and sleep! Lucy thought of the cool water stream beside the cottage and, with a start, remembered she had asked Tage to meet her there after dark. *I'm so thirsty.*

With her mind set on escaping to the cottage where she would be able to rest, and where Lothar would eventually find her, Lucy swiveled the stone outwards and pushed the bag and the stave to fall to the ground beneath. Sliding hands first from the channel, Lucy lay shaking from the agony of her injured leg, moaning with each breath she expelled. She was faint and unaware of minutes slipping away as her senses drifted into a void.

The sensation that she was falling into a bottomless abyss caused Lucy to rouse, but it was some minutes before she became fully aware of where she was and how she had half-climbed, half-fallen from the opening above. Distant shouting brought Lothar to her thoughts, but as she tried to stand, she found it impossible, even with the help of the stave. Rising to a sitting position and leaning against the wall, she felt her leg, trying to see it, but even in the bright shafts of moonlight, her eyes refused to focus on her injury. Wet tackiness on her swollen calf told Lucy she was bleeding. Some of the blood had congealed and, by the size of the swelling, she wondered again if it was broken. Memories of Tage's leg, broken in the same place, came to her mind. As Lucy remembered how it had mended crooked, she realized she was shivering.

The air is not chilly, she told herself, *I'm trembling from shock. If only I could find somewhere safe, then I could sleep.*

Shouts surged louder, deep voices penetrating the night air, and Lucy knew she must find somewhere to hide. *I could climb back in the channel to hide, and wait...* The thought was most unwelcome. *I'll leave my bag. Then Lothar will know I managed to escape, but that I did not go far.*

Lucy forsook any notion of walking to the cottage. She could not stand upright, let alone walk to the other side of the city, and then out to Lord Tullus' estate.

Foraging in the carry-bag, Lucy pulled out her moneybag, then closed and tied the carry-bag. Leaving it, Lucy mustered her strength and raised herself high enough to close the channel. The shouts grew stronger, circling ominously in her spinning head.

I must hide! Visions of Ludwig finding her brought movement. Painstakingly crawling with one leg, dragging the other behind, supporting herself awkwardly with the stave, she pulled herself across the narrow alley and into the shadow of the tall city wall where the alley widened. Earth, instead of stone, was now beneath her, and tall weeds grew near the wall.

Pressing her way behind the weeds, Lucy succumbed to the exhaustion threatening to consume her, and she collapsed into unconsciousness.

Almost half an hour passed before Lucy roused. Dank, earthy odors slowly brought her torpid senses to awareness. Before she opened her eyes, she fancied she lay in the woods under a tree... *But I went to Verdun, the capital...and...oh, no!* The pain was there again, jolting her into reality, and she struggled to sit.

Memories of the past week flooded her mind, and it seemed that all blood drained from her head as she pushed herself up off the ground, which was cold and a little damp, using her hands for support. She started and turned at the sound of the silver jingling in the moneybag. Gritting her teeth as she twisted to sit, Lucy groped for the bag and sighed with relief when her fingers touched the soft leather. Feeling for her belt, Lucy tied the thong of the moneybag in its place, securing the velvet tightly to prevent the coins jingling.

Some mercenary-minded criminal will not catch me this time, she determined. With the stave's help, she forced herself to stand on one foot, slumping back against the wall, waiting to gain control and balance.

Gingerly testing her injured leg, Lucy found she could place only a little weight on her foot before sharp pain shot up her leg. *It may not be broken...*she felt heartened at this thought. However, she supported the leg with the stave as she took an unsteady step. Looking back at the mausoleum, she thought of her carry-bag. *No, I could not take it far; it will be enough for me to be able to walk at all. But then, there are some things I might need.* She thought of the trunk near the cottage. *The trunk has all I need...and more...and I must leave the bag there so Lothar knows I got out.*

The cottage...Tage...I must go there. Lucy clutched the strong stave, thinking, *I'll go to the livery stables and hire a pony, or a horse and cart...there's enough money to buy one if necessary.* She licked her dry lips, feeling faint and very thirsty. Closing her eyes, she felt herself melting into dark gray clouds that threatened to envelop her. She battled successfully to remain upright, preventing herself from collapsing into coveted rest. She forced herself to walk. Her leg, though no longer numb, throbbed savagely, dispelling any thought of relaxation.

Lucy hobbled laboriously along inside the city wall, leaning on it occasionally for respite. She stole back into the shadows at the sound of horses, and held her breath as two mounted soldiers approached, riding toward the mausoleum. Lucy did not know they were part of the regular city patrol. The apprehensive maiden hunched herself over the stave, gripping it with both hands, supporting her trembling, weak frame; holding her breath as they rode so close she could have reached out and touched their horses.

She hoped the men, glancing abstractly in her direction, would behold an old, bent widow woman, tottering a little, maybe drunk. Although Lucy's golden hair was braided around her head in the manner of a young woman, the color could be taken to be gray in the dark shadow of the wall. Her torn widow clothes, the stave, and her quaint, faltering posture spoke of old age. Besides, she was not acting suspiciously or causing any disturbance and was on a public thoroughfare.

Heaving a deep sigh as the hoof-beats faded, Lucy faltered along until she spied a wide street moving up the rise, away from the wall. Entrances to several narrow lanes and alleys had been passed, but Lucy imagined most of those to be blind alleys, cul-de-sacs. Half of them, it seemed, joined with the street occupied by the livery stables. Due to her weak condition and sore leg, Lucy had no intentions of wasting her energy walking uphill only to arrive at a dead-end! Thus, after she had journeyed some distance along the street, she was heading away from the livery stables.

When a bend in the narrow road turned her south, she decided to retrace her faltering gait, and take the last lane that had inclined in what she hoped was the right direction. Several men on foot had overtaken her, and on the way up the rise, both men and women passed by, moving in the opposite direction. The lane, barely a horse and cart wide and crisscrossed by intersections, snaked between wood and stone houses, their front steps right on the uneven cobblestones. Lucy took a right turn until she was looking at an alley that descended to the outer wall again.

I have gone in a circle! I must find a wider street. The livery stables were on a wider street...and I must remember, I'll come upon the livery stables from the opposite end... She paused to rest, listening to the muffled sound of music and feet tapping in time. Singing voices drifted on the night air, and Lucy envied the comfort of a house and a place to rest her aching leg.

Spicy odors and the mouth-watering smell of cooking meat circulated in the built-up lane as flickering candles and bright lamps shining out of open windows spoke of fellowship and food. Lucy closed her eyes, picturing a sumptuous meal. The frantic barks of a nearby dog energized her weary frame. She was thankful that the sound came from behind closed doors, but quickly resumed her hobble, still hoping to locate the livery stables.

Lucy tried to judge her direction by the full moon, now above the rooftops and lighting her way. *It seems nearly as light as day,* she mused, gladly able to read the name on the door of a house: Nicholas Lucas. *I wonder what would happen if I knocked on the door and asked Mr. Lucas the way to the livery stables?* But she would not take such a risk. *How do I know that Mr. Lucas is not involved with Ludwig?* She shuddered.

Finally, Lucy admitted, *I'm lost, hopelessly lost.* Extending her leg cautiously, unable to bend it at the knee, she sank down on a deserted doorstep, resting again. She felt as if she would die of thirst! *Please, dear Father in Heaven, I need a drink...just a little water. Please, God,* she prayed.

Knowing that the water would not just come to her, Lucy stood, wobbling, until she righted her balance. All else was forgotten in her need to find water.

A small family group approached from the opposite direction, and Lucy would have spoken to the woman who herded five children in front of her, but exhaustion had clouded her thinking. They were passing her by the time Lucy managed to say, "I...I'm thirsty..." The children were chattering, however, and she was unheard.

"I'll race you to the well!" one of the children shouted suddenly, a challenge to his siblings.

"I...can't...race..." Lucy whispered hoarsely, thinking the young lad was talking to her. She turned and followed the direction of the shouting children. A tall, broad-shouldered man strode in the rear of the family group.

The lane led into another narrow thoroughfare. This alleyway, to Lucy's amazement, opened out into a corner of the main square. By the time Lucy crossed to the well, the children had slaked their thirst and the family had moved away.

Although it was evening, the square was still populated, but most people were moving, passing through, walking around or across the great empty paved area.

Having thankfully quenched her thirst by drinking three mugs of the crisp water from the bucket the children had drawn, Lucy would have ripped a piece of fabric from her already torn dress to bathe and bandage her leg but she moved away from the well as a man leading a pony approached, with two youths walking beside him.

Moving to the area where she remembered feeding birds, Lucy looked for an empty seat. To her surprise, they were all occupied. Lucy knew that young travelers often could not afford the fees charged at the inns, and now that the weather was warmer, they chose to sleep outdoors. Only when a curfew was imposed, which was very rare, and in the winter, would the great square be deserted at night.

Sinking down under a tree, Lucy ignored a tethered horse cropping at short grass nearby. She was not in the frame of mind to steal a horse, and she knew its owner would be close. As she expected, mounted soldiers patrolled the area, but they obviously did not expect trouble, for they did not ride near the grassy area.

Here I am, unable to walk another step, but I cannot sleep... Lucy thought, frustrated. The pain in her leg, soft snores from someone on the nearby bench, and thoughts of Lothar: wondering where he was, whether or not he had escaped and had rallied loyal troops, conspired to keep her wide awake.

Lucy prayed for Lothar and for the kingdom. She realized how her recent experiences had caused her to depend upon God. *Oh, God, Heavenly Father, I truly do depend upon you like a Father! There's no one else. Thank you, God, for bringing me to this confidence in you. Thank You for making me feel and know in my heart that you are my helper, and that you'll save Lothar and help us.*

She thought of Tage. *He'll be waiting for me, he'll wonder what's happened, why I'm not there. Dear Father in Heaven, please look after Tage,* she prayed, then added with great urgency, *and Yolanda, Avalyn, Jaybee, and Cinnie.* Remembering the Grand

House where the girls would be, she felt comforted that they were safe.

She relaxed and tried to sleep, but the clinking of the horse's mouth-bit came closer and its acrid breath caused her to draw back as it nuzzled close to her face.

Why do animals like me? She reached out and caressed its nose. The animal obviously enjoyed the attention, and Lucy stroked its neck as it nuzzled into her gray widow's dress, obviously intrigued by the garlic smell. Suddenly drawing back, the horse lifted its head, whinnying in fear.

"What's wrong?" Lucy whispered, sure the animal sensed danger. Skittering, pulling fiercely against the confines of its rope, the beast trembled, listening. Lucy's eyes scanned the square. It was impossible to see all the way across, but as far as she could tell, there was nothing to be concerned about. No horses approaching, no shadowy figures creeping about. She settled back against the tree trunk, holding the stave close, watching the animal standing with its head high and ears pointing forward, on full alert.

The horse neighed and shied at the same time Lucy heard the first explosion. A man sprang from a fixed wooden bench, clumsily unsheathing a dagger as he shook himself from his deep sleep, stumbling as his feet sought a defensive stance. Lurching about, he twirled in an unconvincing circle before relaxing his posture and sheathing his dagger.

Approaching his horse, he spoke in soft tones, "Here, boy, what are you about?"

Lucy was afraid the man would see her, but his eyes roved in other directions. Before he looked her way, another explosion came, followed by several more. People in the square roused, their questioning voices raised and excited.

"Look at that glow...in the sky. What is it?" one deep voice asked. "The palace is that way, isn't it?"

"A fire! A fire!" another squealed.

"Let's go and see!" Enthusiastically, the owner of this voice snatched up a bag and began running across the square towards the road leading to the palace.

Lucy, frowning, stood to her good foot, supported by both the tree and the stave. She wished to follow the procession. She could hear shouts and questions as people ran from homes, others hurrying across the square. She could see a bright glow in the sky. Billowing black smoke rose like clouds, hiding the face of the moon, as more explosions shattered the air.

It might be the palace. I could believe Ludwig would set fire to it, she thought, testing her injured leg, and realizing it was now swollen past her knee. *I can't walk even that far.* Sitting down again, she sighed at the relief from sharp pain. *I'll rest here...I can get another drink, and in the morning I'll see if I can make it out to Tullus Hall.*

Lucy strained her ears, listening, but there were no more explosions.

She settled back against the tree, feeling drained and tired.

Her eyes closed, and she wished she could sleep.

Chapter Twenty-three

A faint plaintive melody ascended the night air, and then fell before rising again to a climax. Lucy sat forward, alert. The whistling ceased then began again, growing louder, and Lucy knew that it originated from only one person: Tage. It was a tune he had frequently whistled back in Passcau, and she had often accompanied him.

Softly at first, Lucy joined the whistle, but she was unable to hold enough breath to whistle consistently. Her father had never allowed her to whistle in his presence. "A whistling woman is as a crowing hen; of use to neither God nor men," her father used to say.

But Tage had taught her to whistle and, deciding after her parents' deaths that she would never be of use to God nor man anyway, she had continued in the 'vice' of whistling. A whistling widow was even more shunned, which had made Lucy very happy when she traveled to deliver their embroidery, wearing her disguise and sounding out a bright melody.

Tage paused in his whistling, but the tune faltered on. The melody was erratic, but Tage knew it was "their song." In his excitement, he was unable to continue whistling as he hurried towards the wavering music, knowing from whom it came. "Lucy! Lucy, it's really you," Tage whispered, crouching beside the form that half sat, half lay, under the tree. "What is it?" She clutched at him, weeping. He looked around, but not a soul was to be seen. "Did you see the fire? I saw it after I entered the gates. It must be over the other side of the city." He waited for her sobs to subside, embarrassed that she hugged him and cried into his shoulder. Lucy had never before showed affection toward him.

Placing a protective arm around her, he said, "I've gone to the cottage most nights, in case you returned. Lord Tullus said it was a good idea. He hoped 'Winnie' would come back. The only problem was that he always sent guards with me, and I knew you wouldn't like that, so I said I wouldn't go with them tonight."

Tage drew a deep breath, and then continued, "I went to my room early and waited for the guards to return, then I walked to the cottage. When you didn't come, I decided to whistle my way to the city square and back. If you were somewhere along the way..." Tage stopped, waited, and then asked, "Why didn't you come? Is something wrong?"

"I...I've hurt my leg," Lucy said, wishing to downplay her pain, "it's painful and I can hardly even hobble."

"Where?" Tage demanded. "Show me."

Raising her torn skirt to her knee, Lucy said, "It's my left leg. I don't think it's broken. Be careful Tage, it hurts." She felt his hand on her ankle. The smoke moved away from the moon's face and revealed Lucy's injury in shafts of moonlight penetrating through the leaves and branches of the tree.

Tage grimaced. "You have a gash, your leg is swollen. The blood has dried and it looks horrible. Who did this? Was it a sword?" When Lucy didn't answer, he asked, "Was it a horse's hoof?"

Lucy muffled a strangled sob, which sounded to Tage like a laugh.

"This is no laughing matter, Lucy!" Tage reprimanded, his voice a mixture of fear and authority. He felt Lucy's brow. "You're feverish...and no wonder. When did you eat last?"

"I...I'm not sure...but I had water from the well." Lucy was overwhelmed with the reality of Tage's presence. "Oh, Tage, I'm so glad you are here! You're an answer to my prayers. Stay with me. I can't walk far, but we'll be safe here till morning. How...how are the girls?"

"They're very well, and happy; but missing you, of course," Tage said gruffly. "You need a doctor to tend that leg. I..." He glanced around the square as if regaining his direction. Looking back at her, he asked, "Can you stand enough to lean on me and walk a little way?" She didn't answer, and he added, "Do you have money?"

"Yes."

"Then give it to me. I'll go fetch Doctor Skerry's horse and cart, and then I'll take you to him."

Lucy's trembling fingers would not do her bidding at first, and it took some time to undo the thong of her moneybag, which she handed to Tage.

"Now, don't move. I'll be back as fast as I can. You can tell me about it all later." Tage said, kissing her forehead.
The moonlight disappeared and, when it materialized again, Tage was gone.

***

Tage arrived back in the square with an old horse pulling a small cart. He directed the animal to the grassy area where the four trees grew tall and proud, stretching limbs across their small domain.

Dismounting and tethering the animal to a branch, Tage said, "Doctor Skerry and his son Jeffrey are both on an urgent house call, but Helma—Jeffery's wife—was there and I told her my cousin has hurt her leg. She said to take you there and she'll tend to it."

Tage helped Lucy stand and she leaned on him for support as he drew her to walk a few steps. When they reached the back of the cart, he hoisted her into his arms, lifting her up to sit on the tray. His swift, sure action took her by surprise.

"How did you do that?" she asked.

"You are like a feather, almost weightless," Tage told her, and moved to mount the horse.

"And you are strong!" Lucy called, knowing he would be honored by the compliment. *It's true,* she thought. *Tage is strong, and it's more that just physical strength.*

Settling back against the cart's sideboard, Lucy clenched her teeth at the relentless pain in her leg, seeking to brace herself for a bumpy ride. But it was not the ordeal she expected.

Tage, concerned about Lucy's injury, left the reins loose, allowing the horse to walk slowly. The docile creature moved away from potholes and mounds, walking around the square and down a wide street, traveling east, obviously knowing its way home.

A small stable stood behind the doctor's house, where a young groom waited. Tage carried Lucy up the back steps and into the doctor's house. The young woman, Helma, led them to a waiting room where several wide wooden benches lined the walls.

"Here, let me look," Helma said as Tage helped Lucy sit on a bench. Setting a lamp on the floor, she lifted Lucy's skirts to view the leg wound. "My word indeed, you *have* hurt your leg." She clicked her tongue. Bringing a footstool, she carefully positioned Lucy's leg to rest on it. "When did you eat last?" Helma asked.

Lucy frowned, closing her eyes, trying to remember. Helma answered the question herself, saying, "There's some beef tea in the kitchen. I'll have our cook heat some for you while I fetch a foot tub and we can clean that wound and see what it's really like." She turned to Tage and said, "You can help me, lad."

Tage reentered the room, carrying the foot-tub containing cold water. "How do you feel?" he asked, sitting beside her. He felt her forehead. It was clammy.

"I told Helma that I thought you had a fever, and she agreed. She said your leg could be broken. Doctor Skerry is an expert at setting broken bones. I came here to see him one day, and he said he could fix *my* leg."

Tage sat silent for a while, not wanting to tell his cousin that Doctor Skerry had said his leg would have to be broken again to be straightened. He realized his words had brought no response from Lucy, so he continued, "Helma said that if your leg is broken, it'll be harder to mend due to the wound as well. How did it happen?"

Again, Lucy did not answer.

Helma came back carrying a pottery tub. Sprinkling a fistful of salt into it, she said, "This will help clean the wound." She then spoke to Tage, "There's some water ready for you to bring."

A half-mug of beef tea was brought before the tub was ready and Lucy hungrily sipped the hot spicy soup-like liquid. "Mmm... That was good, thank you," Lucy said, leaning back on the fat cushions Helma had placed behind her back. The tea made her feel strangely untroubled. She tried to think of the prince, wanting to worry about him, but a delicious blankness misted her mind. She closed her eyes.

Tage poured the pitcher of hot water into the tub, staring down at Lucy. Helma had told him she had put some medicine in the beef tea that would ease Lucy's pain. Helma said she did not want Lucy to eat anything, because food combined with the medicine could make her sick. But with liquid only, it worked like a soporific.

Helma had also said that when the doctor arrived, the patient would be asleep and he could deal with her leg. Meanwhile, she would wash it and do as much as she could to make Lucy comfortable and keep her still.

She very gently sponged Lucy's leg, softly clicking her tongue as she did so. Tage sat beside his cousin, averting his eyes from the horrible gouge in Lucy's calf.

"I'm using barely warm water," Helma told him. "Hot water would cause this kind of wound to bleed again. I'm please it's clotted, I am. Obviously, it didn't sever an artery."

Helma's in-depth commentary bothered Tage, and he was glad that Lucy, though whimpering now and then, was oblivious of the woman's colorful descriptions about how bad the injury could have been.

"The doctor will have to stitch it as soon as he comes. It'll leave a scar, though, even then." Helma clicked her tongue and added, "Maybe I'll send for Jeffrey. He can stitch it, and he may not be as needed where he is as he's needed here." She stood and faced Tage. "I'll make a bed ready and you can help me carry your cousin there. What did you say her name is?"

"Lucretia. I've been staying out at the Grand House with Lord Tullus and we'll both return there when the doctor is finished." He was glad Helma was too involved with her own thoughts to realize Lucy's name was of any significance.

"She won't be going anywhere on that leg for a few weeks. No wonder you had to get the cart to fetch her, she couldn't have walked on it." Helma did not wait for Tage to comment, but said, "Help me turn her on her back." She wrapped Lucy's leg with a dry towel.

To Tage's surprise, the bench-top lifted off its sturdy leg-frame, converting into a wooden pallet. Helma had already opened the doors, and she carried the head of the bench-top, moving backwards along a narrow corridor. Tage could tell that the strong young woman had done this many times before.

After sending the groom to inform the doctors that a patient awaited their urgent attention, Helma prepared Lucy for bed, while Tage sipped a mug of beef tea.

"If your cousin is a widow, then I'm a donkey!" Helma declared as she bundled Lucy's torn gray dress together with the bloodstained white muslin dress.

Tage quickly thought of an appropriate reply. "You are right, Helma: you're not a donkey. My cousin has never been married. It...the gray dress...it was...a relative's." He stared at Lucy's waxen appearance. "She'll be all right, won't she?"

The woman placed a hand on Tage's shoulder, saying, "Not a worry, lad! A few days rest with some nourishment and she'll be on the mend." She turned her full attention to the boy. "You look like you could do with a good night's sleep. If you want, I'll fetch a rug and you can bunk down on the bench out there."

Tage did not protest as Helma bustled off. He knew that it was late; he normally would have been asleep by now. He would return to the Grand House before dawn, so they would not miss him.

While the young doctor's wife was gone, he took a silver ducat from Lucy's moneybag, which he had placed on his own belt, and when he tendered the silver coin to Helma, she accepted it readily.

"Jeffrey's father will be well pleased. We do not receive our due often." She looked up at Tage with new interest, her eyes scanning his clothes. "You said your name was Melville, You're not that young lord they're all saying has returned from Cher, are you? Yes, of course you are. Lucretia shall remain here until she's completely recovered. That way, she'll get the best care.

"We use the rooms for confinements, or those who need extra care like your cousin. A bit like a small hospice, but we have no other patients here now; 'cept we might have that young mother that Father and Jeffrey have gone to help. She should have been brought here before she got in such difficulties with her confinement."

Tage was not sure what a confinement was, but he was too tired to ask. He supposed it was some type of ailment that confined one to a bed. The young mother must be more ill than Lucy, he supposed. He soon fell asleep on the bench, having asked Helma to wake him when Doctor Skerry arrived.

But Helma did not awaken Tage when the younger doctor, Jeffery, arrived after midnight. He took care of Lucy's leg, stitching and bandaging it after deciding that it was badly bruised, not broken. "At the worst, the bone has somehow been crushed."

"Crushed?" Helma asked, "How?"

"It was pressed with something crushing with a spear-like protrusion," Jeffrey told his wife, who assisted him. "You must make sure she remains in bed. She must rise for nothing. Father will want to look at her leg tomorrow, and want her to stay here until we remove the stitches next week."

Jeffrey continued, "This confinement could take up to twelve hours or more. We're not sure if the young mother will live, and we have less hope for the babe. It's difficult, really difficult." Not pausing to inquire further about Tage or Lucy, Jeffrey left to return to his previous patient.

Chapter Twenty-four

Tage woke half-an-hour before dawn. At first, he wondered where he was. On the floor?

Rolling over, he discovered he wasn't on the floor...yet! He fell off the bench. *Thud!* The room was dark, and he fought to untangle himself from a woolen rug. Standing, he rubbed his banged elbow and tried again to recall his location. It finally came to him: the doctor's residence in Verdun.

Lucy is here, he thought, wondering how she fared. Winding the rug into a slipshod ball, he tossed it to the bench and felt his way around the other waiting-room benches, seeking to gain his sense of direction. Fumbling a little as he moved along the corridor, his hands found the slightly open door leading into the room where his injured cousin lay. Gingerly pushing the door back, he exhaled in satisfaction as light from a small lamp lit up the womanly figure of Helma sitting beside Lucy's bed.

Smiling a thin smile, Tage was thankful that the woman was earning the silver ducat.

Helma was a light sleeper and had leapt awake at the thud from Tage's fall from the bench.

She lifted her forefinger to her puckered lips as she stood and placed her ample arm about Tage's shoulders. She drew him from the room, pulled the door to, and moved them along the corridor.

"She has a fever. Just a small one, mind, but she imagines herself to be trapped in some place like a graveyard, with daggers, dead bodies and little marble statues! She acted as if trying to hide someone there. Imagine such a dream! Lately, she's been rambling on about the palace, and guards, and swords, and even a handsome prince who was in danger. 'Tis quite astounding, it is, what the mind can invent. Your cousin won't be going anywhere, not for a while."

"I must return to my sisters, they'll be worried," Tage said.

Both started as a loud moan came from Lucy's room. Helma hurried back and Tage watched her push Lucy back down on the bed and sponge her hot brow, speaking in soothing tones. After straightening the tossed bedclothes, she waited until Lucy slept, then stepped to Tage's side.

"She'll be restless until the fever abates." Helma frowned suddenly, then asked, "You have sisters?" She did not wait for Tage to speak, but demanded, "Bring one or two of them to sit with her. They'll be needed. I have plenty else to do.

"I can't be here every moment and the next two days will be painful for her and she must be kept in bed." The woman's hand flew to her temple and she clicked her tongue, saying, "You'd better make haste about it. My husband said it's rumored that Prince Lothar, the king-elect, was murdered yesterday. He said it's difficult to find out exactly what's going on. With the old king being dead, the city will likely be in a state of disarray, especially if the prince is truly dead, too."

"I heard there was an attempt on the prince's life, but I didn't know he had died..." Tage began, alarmed at the news.

"Well, no bells have been rung, and no curfew has been ordered, but Jeffrey said there have been soldiers coming and going at the palace all night. Several disturbances with swords being used. And he saw several fatalities lying along the way. The city will be no place to linger. You just hurry up and bring your sisters."

Tage nodded. "We have a nurse named Cynthia. I'm sure she'll want to come, and Yolanda, she's twelve, she'll be most willing to help..."

Lucy groaned again and Helma turned toward her. Lucy had only tossed the bedclothes back this time. Her eyes were still closed and she remained on her back.

"Then make haste. I'll be glad of all the help you can bring, that I will, if things are as unsettled as Jeffrey says."

Clicking her tongue again, she pressed Tage's shoulder as though to turn him away, then said, "Wait. Wake Fin, the stable boy. He sleeps in the loft. Help him get the horse and cart ready. That way, you'll be able to return sooner, and your sister and the nurse can ride on the cart."

Tage was sure that Lord Tullus would send a carriage for Yolanda and Cynthia, but he thought of the distance to the Grand House and knew the horse would indeed save time on the outward journey.

"I'll be glad of just the horse, thank you, Helma." Tage hurried away.

Fin was slow to wake. Muttering that he had suffered a broken night worse than usual, Fin pointed Tage in the direction of the stable and turned over on the straw, pulling his thin blanket over his bony shoulders.

Tage was not going to be brushed away by the sleepy lad. "Wake up! I need your help to find a saddle for the horse. I need it to fetch extra help for Doctor Skerry's patient. Shall I report your laziness to the Doctor?"

Fin was up immediately and climbed down the wooden ladder. Stretching and yawning, but without speaking, he helped Tage saddle the old horse.

Streaks of yellow brightening the navy-blue sky greeted Tage as he urged the horse around the Verdun Square. He frowned at the sight of two bodies, obviously soldiers, on the other side of the street leading towards the palace. A group of four youths, about Tage's age, were arguing over the boots and jackets of the dead men. Other residents were gathering into groups, discussing the state of affairs.

Tage urged the horse toward the west gate, but hesitated at the sight of a mounted company coming from the palace, formatting two across the road. He halted the old animal and drew back, waiting until the horses had ridden past him. As the sky burst with sunlight, the company sped up and disappeared into the gap beside the high city wall, the same gate through which Tage intended to exit.

Following from a safe distance, he mused, *I picked up a phobia about red uniforms from Cher, but I must remember the enemy then wore a much deeper red, almost the color of blood.*

Tage dug his heels into the horse's fat sides, urging the old creature into a lazy canter.

There was the sound of a battle ahead, horses and military in disarray, cavalry turning with foot soldiers in pursuit, and horses galloping back towards Tage. Caught between the wall and dwellings, he could only turn his beast and ride back the way he had come. Urging the old animal on as fast as it could move, Tage hoped for a side street to duck into so he could allow the retreating company to pass.

Helma was right: the city was in disarray! Tage's heart beat faster when mounted soldiers appeared ahead of him now, approaching quickly. The company behind him was gaining, riding swiftly back from the gate.

I'm in the middle of a war! Tage thought, his bravery fleeing rapidly. He was plagued by undesired memories of the battle in Cher, where his leg had been broken by a vicious mace strike.

A bell began to toll, an over-riding, distinctive sound, and was soon joined by others. A horseman cantered towards him, slowing his horse and shouting, "A state of emergency has been declared! Get back where you came from! Enemies of the throne are in the palace! It's not safe out of doors!"

Tage pulled his horse to the side of the street, allowing the man, still shouting his message, to ride past. As Tage once again urged the horse into a canter, he noticed residents opening their peepholes, their faces and eyes peering out of gates and doors, only to slam them shut again at the sounds of the street battle and whinnying horses.

Fearful, the lad looked back to see that he was barely ahead of the battle, the sounds of sword on sword, frightened horses, and human cries and curses, pursuing him closely. Tage's heart pounded erratically, all but drowning out the pealing bells in his ears. Ahead, he saw red uniforms, a street cordon blocking the street.

Seeing no other way, he reluctantly dismounted. "Go home," he shouted, slapping the horse's rump. "Go home."

He ducked into a very narrow alley, praying it wasn't a dead-end, hobbling as fast as he could on his lame leg. In all the confusion, he had lost his sense of direction.

The nebulous sound of battle spurred him on. He was sure he was being followed, even though he chose alleys too narrow for a horse. Heavy running boots behind him spoke of trouble that he did not want to be involved in. He searched for an open door—any portal of safety— where he could rest and get his bearings.

Panting painfully as he passed by closed doors and locked gates, Tage finally ducked into a shadowy, strangled alleyway. Knowing it's snake-like path would lead to the back of some residences, he paused at the feel of raw sewerage under his boots, and leaned on the damp wall, closing his eyes, praying that any pursuers would pass by without seeing him. As normal breathing returned, he wondered why he was acting so afraid, as though the plight of the city was his fault.

This fight is not my doing; it has nothing to do with me. Why am I behaving like a field mouse being chased by a large city cat? I should not fear...God is with me! Please, God, help me.

With his prayer, Tage's courage returned somewhat. *I'm not part of this war. Why should they harm me? I will ask someone the way to Doctor Skerry's residence.*

Creeping back to the corner and stretching his neck, Tage scanned the street. The close pealing of the bells made the battle sounds seem even more distant, and he chose to go left, hoping to find the doctor's house. *Or, I could take refuge in the church, one can always find safety there. I will follow the sound of the bells...*

He darted across an intersection, aware of foot soldiers in the distance, moving his way, approaching rapidly. *Maybe I should speak to them,* he thought, but lost his courage again as he recalled the Cher battle. *This is another Cher, except this time it is amongst the soldiers of Lotharingia. Maybe it's true, Prince Lothar has been murdered and this is a battle for the throne.*

Choosing a wider street, Tage drew his breath when he realized that the church of the 'old faith' lay ahead of him. His pace increased for a few seconds, then slowed. Something was wrong. Smoke was seeping from every crevasse in the great cathedral. The church had been set on fire! There was a loud explosion and flames leapt into sight.

Still, the bells tolled, mixing with the echoes of battle, cries and shouts circling in air charged with strife. Tage moved backwards as the church doors were flung open and four priests hurried out, followed by three monks. The bell overhead slowed and died as flames leapt high, putting the other buildings at risk.

Soldiers raced along the street and Tage flattened himself against a door, aware of eyes peering out through the grate. He breathed a sigh of relief when soldiers passed by him without a glance.

After a quick conference with the priests, the soldiers entered the burning building, only to retreat swiftly.

A priest shouted, "They set it on fire and escaped out the back way! Said they'll burn all of Verdun's churches before they're done! Traitors against God and the throne."

The soldiers lined up before their captain, awaiting orders.

"Have the residents bring buckets and form a line to the well. I must report in." He pivoted on his heel as foot soldiers ran toward the church.

The door behind Tage opened and he found a metal urn, full of water, thrust into his hands. A large man shoved him, wordlessly pointing towards the church, giving him no choice but to move ahead of the man's overpowering frame.

Thus Tage found himself part of a water chain, close enough to feel the heat of the burning building, passing buckets, pitchers, bowls, receptacles, until he lost count of time.

Although used to chopping wood, his muscles ached, and he forced himself to support each vessel thrust into his hands. In his weariness, he even forgot the reason he passed the water.

Several times, those at the fore of the chain had to move back from the heat, and soon the focus was moved from the church to the surrounding buildings. Sparks were lodging in roofs, and calls for assistance came from all directions. The number of military increased, and the water chain was reformed, several others passing water to the houses and up ladders to dampen the roofs.

Morning was well gone before Tage found himself unneeded. He moved away, sinking down on a step along with many other tired residents. The fires were dying and countless men in scarlet uniforms now had them under control.

"I hear they set fire to the other churches, including the one of the New Faith, and the chapel near the palace," Tage heard a man say.

"Why did they do it?" a woman asked.

"Seems they have a grudge against everything to do with the Christian faith. They want to turn Lotharingia into...into...a..." He turned to another man, asking, "What was it? To worship the new king they were going to install?"

"Like old Rome, they want it, I heard. The new king will be a deity." The man said.

"Prince Lothar won't have any of that!" the woman exclaimed. "He believes in God like his father! But, what will we all do? Not a church in the city? Where will we worship?"

A fourth voice spoke up, "God is to be worshipped in the heart and the home first, so we'll do it there until the churches are rebuilt." Everyone was silent after this proclamation.

Having caught his breath, rested his aching arms, and accepted food and drink as it was offered, Tage could see that the fires had died right down, but the church was almost razed.

He moved further away from the choking smoke, which now wafted his way. Turning from the scene, Tage asked the direction to Doctor Skerry's residence.

"Take the third turn, left, and you will move north into the street where the doctor resides," a man told him.

As the afternoon was almost gone, Tage decided to make haste back to Lucy. *My cousin could be in danger,* he worried. *Helma said she needs help, but the doctors will be needed out here to take care of the injured. I'm thankful that Yolanda, Avalyn and Jaybee are safe at Lord Tullus's house with Cinnie.*

With buildings being set on fire, who knew what would happen next?

Chapter Twenty-five

Tage turned wearily down the street where Doctor Skerry lived. His smoke-bleary eyes followed the cobblestones beneath his feet. He was so tired, he stumbled and almost fell.

Wood-chopping uses different muscles, Tage mused, and then realized, *I haven't chopped wood for some time, not since we left Passcau. No surprise that I'm getting out of practice. Being a lord has been a rather idle occupation so far...*

He sighed, sure that he was on the street of his destination. He looked up along the way in front of him, and his smile fled, replaced by a deep frown. Eight scarlet-uniformed men stood outside the doctor's dwelling, guards on duty.

Why do I feel afraid? he asked himself. *It's my cousin who's in there, not a criminal. There's no reason for guards to be here, at least not for Lucy's sake. Ah, there must be injured soldiers in there.* Lifting his chin with uncertain courage, he continued toward the doctor's house.

"What are you about?" a guard asked, stepping in front of the lad when Tage turned to walk down the alleyway to the back door. The alley was lined with more tethered horses than Tage could count.

"My cousin was injured, and she's in Doctor Skerry's House. I've come back to help the doctor's wife..." Tage took a backward step.

"There's a curfew on, lad; you must return to your home."

"I...I tried to go out to Tullus Hall, sir, but there was too much trouble in the city. I was waylaid at the church, and made to help on the water-chain."

A second guard stepped closer, asking, "What's your name, boy?"

"Tage, sir. Tage Melville."

"And your cousin is in Doctor Skerry's house? What's your cousin's name?"

Tage colored and swallowed, deciding to tell the truth. "Lucretia, sir. Her name is Lucretia Melville."

"Then you'd better go to your cousin, Lord Melville," the guard said, bowing. "I'm sure she'll be pleased to see you. But use the front door, sir. You might be glad to know the horse you borrowed returned by itself."

Tage climbed the stone steps and entered the front door, held open by one of the soldiers who announced him: "Lord Tage Melville."

The hallway was lined with guards wearing scarlet uniforms. Tage recoiled at the sight, and his mind seemed not to function. He could not reason why so many soldiers occupied the doctor's house. All faces turned his way, and the men bowed. A young soldier hurried to him.

"Sir Melville? Yes! Madam Jeffrey said you'd been here. You're Miss Melville's cousin? She's much improved, her fever has gone down." He smiled at Tage. "I am Sir Leonhard—Leo— Second Brigadier of King Lothar's army. Come, I'll take you to your cousin..."

Tage followed him, frowning deeply. This young soldier could not be Second Brigadier; could he? But his questions were forgotten when he arrived at the room where he had left Lucy.

Opening the door, Leo announced, "Lord Tage Melville."

A stranger sat on the far side of Lucy's bed, her hand held tightly in his. The man did not stand at the announcement, but looked up. His face looked as weary as Tage felt. Tage did not know him and his face flushed at the man's obvious intimacy toward Lucy.

Helma stood at the end of the bed, smiling, but it was obvious she had also been crying.

"Tage..." Lucy held her free hand out to him as he approached slowly. The stranger still held her other hand.

Tage bent to kiss her cheek. “You look much better, Lucy.” A chair was pushed in behind him, and he sat.

“What happened to you? I hope you weren’t in any battles?” Lucy asked. “Your face is sooty, and your clothes...”

“There was a fire at the church. I helped on the water chain...” Tage noticed the stranger look up toward the door where the Second Brigadier still stood.

The stranger stood. “Now that Lord Melville is here, Lucretia, we shall rejoin the troops battling to regain the palace. As I explained, we’re hoping all traitors have fled the city...” He looked lovingly down at Lucy.

To Tage’s amazement, the stranger kissed Lucy right on the lips. It was a gentle kiss, but much more than a brotherly kind of kiss. Tage almost gasped aloud to see Lucy returning the gesture, clutching the man’s hand tightly.

“We *must* go,” the stranger said, unconvincingly.

Lucy released his hand, settling back on the many pillows behind her.

The soldier bowed, and the stranger left the room, Helma curtsying and following him as if spellbound.

Tage demanded, “Who was that man?”

“Oh, Tage...I’m sorry...I should have introduced you...” Lucy smiled, and then asked, “What’s wrong?”

“He...he was familiar with you!” Tage said in indignation. “Who did he think he was? It was not proper at all!”

Lucy smiled. “That was Prince—King—Lothar.” She saw her cousin’s wide-eyed amazement. “He’s the one who asked me to marry him back in Passcau. And he asked me again today, just before you came. Poor Helma cried her eyes out when I asked the prince if he was sure, and then said *yes*. Let me tell you about it.”

Tage listened to the Lucy's story, finding it hard to believe.

Her voice grew tired as she told how the prince discovered she was at Doctor Skerry's house. "Leo...that is, Sir Leonhard, just after you left this morning, brought a cart-load of wounded soldiers here. Just as he was leaving, he remembered my wound and asked Doctor Skerry if he had seen a maiden with a leg injury. The doctor didn't know I was here, since it was his son, Jeffery, who stitched my leg, but Helma overheard and brought Leo to me."

Lucy blushed. "I'm glad Leo doesn't know I was Mary. It makes me awfully embarrassed to think I will have to tell Prince—King—Lothar about Mary. Oh, Tage, I love him so much! I don't believe I existed before I realized I love him."

"So, Sir Leonhard fetched King Lothar, then, after he realized you were the Lucretia they searched for?"

"Yes," Lucy sighed. Closing her eyes, she was silent.

Tage watched her for several minutes and realized she had fallen asleep. Kissing his cousin's forehead lightly, he tiptoed out; jumping when he almost walked into a guard standing outside the door. Hunger overcame his tiredness and he headed for the kitchen, where the cook provided him with a large helping of delicious stew.

Helma bustled in. "I've got a bed-chamber ready for you, Lord Melville. Sir Leonhard said you're to stay here. The curfew will keep on solid until the emergency is over. And don't be alarmed at all them soldiers, the king himself ordered a guard to be placed on our house."

"I'd like to sit with Lucy." Tage said stubbornly. He was so sleepy, he could have fallen asleep right here at the kitchen table. It was long past sunset now.

"No need, Sir Melville, lad. I'm taking the first watch of the night. Jeffrey will be staying in to take care of the soldiers, and we're getting extra help as two women are coming from the Melville, your castle, just as soon as they can be transported here."

Tage almost asked, *My castle?* But he remembered Lucy's story. The Melville was *his* castle! He wondered if he would get used to the idea. Then he thought of his sisters.

"My sisters will be anxious. I didn't get out of the city this morning."

"Don't fret about them," Helma assured him, "Sir Leonhard sent a soldier out with a message that you were in the city and that Miss Lucretia is safely found. Just the northern gate was free, and the messenger would have had to ride right around the long way. Your sisters cannot come until the eastern gate is retaken and everything calms down."

Checking that Lucy was settled for the night, and that Helma was sitting with her, Tage bathed as he had been commanded to by the young doctor's wife, and climbed into one of the guest-bed's in the doctor's residence. It was a four-poster, and most unlike the wooden beds used for patients. He was being treated royally and decided he liked it.

Falling asleep instantly, he slept deeply until the small hours of the morning. He had to rouse himself completely before remembering where he was. Suddenly, a great feeling of thankfulness flooded him and he climbed out of the four-poster bed, to kneel down beside it.

"Thank you, Heavenly Father. Thank you for working everything out. Lucy has found you *and* she has found love. Please help her...help her...*to be a good queen*!"

Overwhelmed with the marvel of it all, Tage could pray no more. Lucy, the queen! He wondered if *she* had considered this amazing reality. No longer sleepy, he pulled his smoke-stained tunic on again, and tiptoed to her room. The guards in the house no longer bothered him but made him feel secure. If any of Ludwig's men were in the city and knew of Lucy's presence here, they would be unable to create a problem.

The room was empty! Tage's heart leapt, and for an instant he wondered if he had dreamed the whole thing.

"Miss Melville has been moved to a guest room, sir" a soldier informed him. "I'll take you there."

Lucy's guest-chamber was in a different wing of the large house and was larger and more comfortable. She was fast asleep, another stranger, a woman this time, sitting beside the bed. The guard did not announce Tage, and he quietly took a chair on the other side of the large four-poster bed, where, leaning forward, he too slept.

***

Lucy was bored of staying in bed so long. She repeatedly asked when her younger cousins were coming, and repeatedly got the same answer: Cynthia would come as soon as the gate was free, and the others would follow as things became more settled.

Four days passed before Cynthia arrived to help care for Lucy.

The palace had been retaken and the city was being returned to law and order. A curfew, however, was still enforced between sunset and sunrise. There were reports of continued skirmishes, deserting soldiers, and arson. Troops from other provinces of Lotharingia arrived and heavy city patrols were organized. Lucy's cousins would have to wait a little longer.

***

Morning and evening, one-page letters, along with bouquets of flowers, arrived from the king-elect. He wrote how much he longed to visit her, but knew she understood how heavily committed he was with the upheaval in the city and the palace. Also, the vigil for his father had to continue. Barons, lords and ladies from the provinces were arriving continuously to pay their respects.

In the fourth letter from the prince, he declared his deep love for her: *I live only for the moment that I can have you by my side forever*, he wrote. *Write and say you will marry me when Father's funeral is over, and I shall be greatly comforted.*

Lucy had never written a letter before, and she found the task all absorbing, her boredom suddenly forgotten. At first, her shyness and reticence blocked her from declaring her love, but it became easier in subsequent letters, where she expressed her love to the king-elect, knowing it was what he wanted and needed. She found herself falling more in love with him and longing to see him again. To love and be loved was a new feeling; she felt as though she floated in the sky.

Yes, yes, yes, a thousand times, yes! I am unworthy of you, but if you please, I will marry you. Forgive me, Your Highness, forever refusing you. I was a different person then, from the one I am now. And Lucy wrote about her experience at Melville Castle, how she had believed in God's Son, Jesus, and had found peace. *I feel sure, that my cousin Tage's prayers have been answered and God is working everything in His great and glorious plan for our lives. I thank Him every moment for our love and for His great patience with me.*

Cynthia fussed around Lucy, excited that, at last, Lucy was known as Lucretia Melville. "King or not; I'll have to see that he's good enough for you, my girl."

"He is everything a man should be," Lucy said. "Kind and compassionate, but still commanding. He makes me feel safe and loved." *Thank You God...he loves me,* she added in a silent prayer.

When Lothar did visit Lucy two days later, Cynthia curtsied low and remained in silent awe to see the tall handsome frame bend to kiss her beloved Lucy. It seemed like a beautiful dream-story.

Wearing the same blue woolen bed-shawl Helma had loaned her, Lucy complained how tiresome it was to be in bed so long. "I'm learning more patience; but I find it very hard," she admitted.

"As do I," Lothar said, his eyes sparkling. "I love you very much, Lucretia. I've appointed a court and was able to take counsel. Our wedding should take place in a month." He kissed her hand.

"But, I'm still puzzled about something, Lucretia. Is your mother, Widow Winifred, still alive?" He saw her blush, and continued, his eyes twinkling with humor, "Also, a maid who arrived at the Melville as Mary, but seems to have left as a different maiden with golden braids and wearing a white dress. A guard saw her as she disappeared into the woods.

"And, Lucretia, you wrote to me about being at the Melville, but no one there remembers you..."

Feeling guilty, but glad that only Tage and Cinnie listened, Lucy told Lothar the story of her different disguises. When she had finished, the prince's face grew unusually stern.

"I've upset you," Lucy bowed her head. "And you're right to be ashamed of me. What I did was unthinkable."

Lifting her chin so she looked into his eyes, he said, "Don't even try to imagine that I'm ashamed, Lucretia. I'll never be ashamed of you. Indeed, I'm proud, very proud. Your widow disguise saved my life in the palace...and, without Mary, how would you ever have known Tobie? I'm concerned that you have braved such dreadful odds all alone. I shudder to imagine...Tobie..."

He was silent for a moment and then said, "I'm not sure how I will manage all three women."

For a moment, Lucy was despondent, then, as she saw the glints in his eyes and the slight twitch of his lips, she knew he was teasing. "Which woman would you wish to marry, then, Sire?" she asked coyly.

"There is only one for me, and that is Lucretia Melville. But we shall definitely have to ban wiggery and maskery." he said firmly.

"Wiggery?—Maskery?" she asked.

"The wearing of wigs and masks will be banned forever," he declared. "I want only to look at your lovely golden hair and your face for the rest of my life. No gray wigs. And definitely, *no masks*."

He smiled. "Lucretia, you are the key to my love."

"And you are the key to my love, Sire."

"Not Sire, but Lothar."

"Then I shall be Lucy," she declared.

"Ah, but you will always be Lucretia to me. *Queen* Lucretia," he challenged her, and his eyes sparkled. He kissed her hand again and looked into her eyes, adding, "But, sometimes I shall have other names for you."

"Other names?" she asked innocently.

"Like 'Darling' and, 'Sweetheart'. One life-time will not be long enough to tell you and show you how much I love you." He kissed her on the lips.

Across the room, Tage whispered in Cynthia's ear, "This is getting mushy."

She pushed him away, wiped the tears from her eyes, and whispered back, "Just you learn something, Tage boy, uh, Sir. One day you'll find your key."

"Key? What key?"

"When love is given by one and returned by another, it's a circle that goes on eternally. And it's the key to what we all desire. It's the Key to Love."

"Yes," Tage said, remembering and smiling. "The Key to Love."

PORTRAITS OF LOVE
The Melvilles

KEY TO LOVE is the first complete story about the Melvilles of Lotharingia, and deals with Lucretia Melville and the King of Lotharingia.

SPEAK TO THE HEART is about Yolanda Melville and the Queen and King of Polav.

TOUCH THE SKY is about Avalyn Melville and King Roswell of Rosenburg.

Story four will be about Tage Melville
and his search for his 'true love.'

Story five will be about Jane-Belle Melville.

Each is a complete and stand-alone story.

Stories that are much more than just stories...

Contact the author:

Carolyn Ann Aish: carolyn.aish@xtra.co.nz

Other stories set in by-gone eras
By Carolyn Ann Aish:

Fleeing Shadows
A Treasure Store
Kind Heart
Stepping Stones
Key to Love
Touch the Sky
Angel Hands
Sing of Love
The Frencolian Chronicles Series:
Book 1, A Chosen Love
Book 2, A Daughter's Love
Book 3, A Brother's Love
Book 4, Treasures
Book 5, Castles
Book 6, Kingdoms
Coming:
Book 7, Secrets
Book 8, Slaves
Also:
Selina's Secret

Much MORE than just stories...

www.ingramcontent.com/pod-product-compliance
Lightning Source LLC
LaVergne TN
LVHW080248110826
845148LV00023BA/827
* 9 7 8 1 8 7 7 2 1 9 8 1 8 *